# Lief 1

# Lesser and

# Hell

By Robin Bennett

Lief the Lesser and Hell (Monster Books).

Originally published in Great Britain by Monster Books, The Old Smithy, Henley-on-Thames, Oxon. RG9 2AR.

Published May 2023

A catalogue record of this book is available from the British Library.

*Doggerland was the prosperous and powerful kingdom that connected Britain to Europe 8,000 years ago. But from great beginnings, it now lies drowned; lost forever, far below the cold waves of the North Sea. Its disappearance was caused by a great tsunami. And what about the people who lived in Doggerland? More importantly, what about the survivors?*

## Prologue: Doggerland

[BARD]

*Come! Hear my song of long before,*
*There was no sea, there was no shore.*
*Just rolling hills and fields of grass,*
*That moved like waves in pastures vast.*
            *But this was very soon to pass.*

*Come! Hear my song of Lief and Hell,*
*And of what became that time will tell.*
*They roamed the hills and slipped through*
*grass,*
*Like parting waves in pastures vast.*
            *But this was very soon to pass.*

*Lief loved his father and his mother,*
*Hell quite alone, save her brother.*
*Each dwelt in strongholds, daunt and fast,*
*That rose from hills on pastures vast.*
            *But this was very soon to pass.*

*And though they shared these land-locked*
*seas,*
*Lief and Hell were enemies.*
*But hate will wane and love outlast,*
*The floods that rush through pastures vast*

            *… and this was very soon to pass.*

everything else in the stone tower where they lived.

'Perhaps today, but I'll grow and I'll be a warrior!' Lief retorted. Hell snorted rudely.

'Why would you want to be one of those oafs? Anyway, you're too small and your destiny is different … I can see.'

'No you can't, you just pretend to have Second Sight.' Lief was trying not to get annoyed but Hell always went on about this destiny stuff. Besides Lief knew that if you couldn't fight, you didn't have much of a place in the village and that worried him. 'I'll grow … like my father.'

'What, fat?'

'He's not!' Lief was angry now. Lief's father had been the best fighter in the village, and their chief – until he'd taken an axe blow to the head during a raid. Now he sat at home most of the time and slept. 'He *is* a warrior.'

'Used to be, now he's a big ball of lard who's scared of his own shadow. He's a worrier.'

Lief felt himself going very red; Hell was looking triumphant. She always found a way to make him lose his temper. He hated her. Really. Hated. Her.

'At least I've got a father!' Then as soon as he'd said it, he wished he hadn't.

Hell went pale.

*Paler*.

She blinked hard in the sunlight. Why me? thought Lief. There were other kids whose lives she could make miserable. But deep down he knew why: Lief and his family were the only people in the village who would actually talk to Hell and her brother, who were orphans and therefore outcasts.

'Look … I'm sorry …' He really didn't feel like it but he stepped towards her. He'd known Hell all his life but she only sought him out in order to find new ways to make him feel pointless. He just wanted her to leave him alone … then again, he shouldn't have said what he had. Hell had covered her face and was shaking. He sort of waved his hand a few inches above her shoulder. 'Um … there, *there*?' he said. He wished he was anywhere else right now, even cleaning out the pigs. 'I didn't …'

A small bony fist shot up and hit him – right on the end of his nose. *Aargh*! Lights went off in his head and tears welled up in his eyes. He would have given everything he had in the whole world to stop them. But that wasn't the way it worked – you got hit on the nose: tears came. It wasn't proper crying, but still … and Hell was laughing, not sobbing.

'Oh! boo hoo: Lief got hit by a girl and now he's going to run off and tell his mummy.' Hell drew herself up to her full height. 'Go on, run away, like you always do …'

Lief started to turn. Tears were running down his cheeks and he didn't want his father to see – normally he'd go to the creek and sulk. But he stopped: not today. A stick lay at his feet and he reached down. Hell's face went from triumphant to alarmed.

'Gan var deeth voll deg …' She started moving her fingers chanting in the Old Tongue.

'Stop pretending you're a witch.' Lief picked up the stick, which was heavy and gnarled and moved towards her: yet somewhere, in the back of his mind, he registered the birds had stopped singing.

'Gan thargh mell koll quin steg dar kill!'

Lief raised the stick but paused because a wind had sprung up from nowhere. It raced across the grasslands, laying the bronze-coloured stems flat, and a roaring sound built in the distance, very faint and very far – but that meant it must be very loud to carry such a way.

Had Hell called up a storm?

Something huge had just appeared on the horizon, all the way from one end of it to the other: grey and tumbling, like a low storm cloud topped white. The increasing roar, that wasn't coming from the wind but perhaps the grey wall, got louder. The stick dropped from his hands.

'I knew you wouldn't dare!' Hell looked triumphant. Then puzzled. Lief was not even listening – he was staring over her shoulder …

Lief swallowed hard, but his mouth felt full of ash: *water* was rushing towards them … more than he had ever seen, more than he knew existed.

'What have you done?' murmured Lief.

[BARD]
*Hell turned and saw, ten fathoms high,*
*A wall of water at land-meets-sky,*
*As far across as any eye.*
*'Gods,' she cried, 'we're going to die.'*

*Stampeding beasts now thundered by,*
*A flock of birds took to the sky,*
*Yup, thought Lief, we're going to die,*
*I think I know the reason why.*

'This is completely and utterly all your fault!' shouted Lief over the rumble of hooves as a herd of roe deer narrowly missed them. For the first time in her life, Hell looked shocked and scared.

'I didn't do anything! I just made up some words, I …'

'Whatever … we've got to warn the others!'

'We're too late!'

*A wave a hundred leagues at least*
*Swallowed them – the ravenous beast!*
*– mere morsels, for It craved a feast:*
*That meal was Doggerland.*

*Suddenly there was no sound,*
*No up, no down, but all around*
*was water, panic, nowhere ground,*
*That once was Doggerland.*

*And just when he was sure to die,*
*Lief surfaced 'neath the tarry sky,*
*Behind him he then heard a cry,*
*And that was Hell at hand.*

*Who sat upon a gnarly tree,*
*That floated on this nasty sea.*
*'There's nothing left but you and me!*

*For gone is Doggerland!'*

*But as he held on fast and grimly,*
*Lief spied his parents, on a chimney,*
*And Hell's brother, very dimly,*
*For night was close at hand.*

*They waved and waved.*
*'That's it we're saved!*
*Our home is lost but we have braved,*
*The scourge of Doggerland.'*

*But cruel currents took the tree,*
*Away from home and family*
*– a lonely way, far out to sea.*
*Away from Doggerland.*

## Chapter 1: Adrift

'It was me, it was me, it was me, it was me, it was me.' Hell had been staring at her hands for the last hour, her fingers twisting around themselves. Lief sat at the other end of the log, as far away as he could get without falling off into the swirling, dark waters. He watched her carefully.

'I don't think it was you,' he said eventually. Hell's intense gaze turned on him but she said nothing. 'If your spell really worked, surely it would have harmed me? I was the one threatening you. Instead, it got everyone else.' By way of a reply, Hell shrugged.

'I don't care about them.'

'I can't believe you'd say that about the others in the village … my parents … you really don't care about anyone!' he shouted, stress suddenly making him angry, out here in all the confusing darkness … then Lief slumped: he was too tired and too worried to think about Hell. For the last few hours, they'd seen no sign of land or anything other than the choppy, cold waters swirling around them, full of dark shadows, like the spirits of the drowned. Apart from a few frightened animals swimming past, eyes white with fear, and debris from their village that swept past as they held onto the tree, everything had been washed away or smothered by the wall of water.

However, anger directed at Hell almost felt good; it took his mind off his fear and confusion.

It felt real when nothing else did.

But it didn't help his queasy stomach that lurched and swayed as much as the log they clung to. Humans were not meant to ride water, he'd decided after the third time he'd coughed up the contents of his stomach. He swallowed yet another mouthful of watery acid and spoke through clenched teeth. 'It wasn't you, something went wrong; I've never seen so much water and I doubt anything like that has ever happened, maybe the gods were angry with us about something, but small people like us …'

' … mmm,' muttered Hell under her breath as if that, at least, she could agree with.

'… like *all* of us, including you – we don't know what the gods are thinking any more than …' he paused: in the light of the full moon, Hell had picked an earwig out of the tree and was studying it, '… any more than that earwig knows what we're talking about.' Hell, whose stomach didn't seem to be affected by the movement of the water, looked across at Lief and, very deliberately, popped the wriggling insect in her mouth, then chewed. Lief looked at her levelly. 'Eating insects does not make you cool and interesting. It makes you look disturbed.'

Hell shrugged. 'They're good, my brother and I eat them when he can't hunt.' She spat something out of the corner of her mouth. 'The heads are bitter.'

'Still revolting,' said Lief.

'Which just means I'll survive on this journey and you'll starve.'

'What? No – no I won't! And what do you mean *journey*? As soon as it gets light we'll see where we are and we can probably turn this thing around and go back the way we came … or … or all this water will have drained away by then and we can walk home.' Lief desperately wanted to go back and find his parents, but he refrained from saying so – he knew Hell wouldn't understand or she would be scornful. Hell had been on her own most of her life. She was used to it. He wasn't. 'We can't have gone that far.' There was a longish pause.

'You think so?' Hell had a manic glint in her dark eyes. Lief swallowed, she could look quite scary sometimes. 'You *really* think so?'

[HELL]
*They whisper to each other in the deep,*
*Where they lie away from light,*
*Their bodies float, as if to sleep,*
*Their skin is waxy white.*

she started to chant.

In spite of himself, Lief began to slap the wooden trunk in time with the beat, like the adults did when the bards sang their stories late at night. And right now, stuck on this log, in the dark and freezing cold, he was desperate for something that was anything like home.

*The drowned battalions of the dead,*
*Shall soon awake and rise.*
*A zombie prince rides at their head,*
*To claim his living prize.*

Given the circumstances, Lief would have preferred something more cheerful.

*Out they'll march this salty sea,*
*To trudge upon dry land,*
*Their ranks a reeking potpourri,*
*Their goal is close at hand.*

*They'll fall upon our living flesh,*
*Suck out our tongues and eyes,*

16

*They like us warm, they like us fresh,*
*Tucked up in beddy-byes.*
*They'll chomp away and chew ...*

'OK! This has been *Great*!' he said, before he had to listen to any more. 'I know!' Hell reluctantly glanced up at him, 'let's keep completely quiet until it's daylight.'

## Chapter 2: Albion

[BARD]
*Dark waters,*
*Secret slaughters.*

*The Moon stared*
*at crashing waves of crushing danger,*
*At a new stranger! ... oh, She glared,*
*Whilst the other gazed back, serene,*
                    *Cool as Nitro-glycerine.*

*This New Moon Imposter,*
*This evil twin, this foster*
*sister, silver blister.*

*Was this shining disk*
*one coin to cross the Styx?*
*Or the door to what was once – but now no*
*more?*

*The Moon turn gazed, full phased,*
*At refuse refugees.*
*Kids-on-a-stick,*
*A candle without a wick ...*
*a light in the darkness.*
*One full Fury, one Less*
*But a light.*

*Nonetheless.*

Lief woke in full-blown shock, as the enormity of what had happened sank in with the sight of endless, grey waves. He felt sicker than he ever had in his life, and his arms and legs ached with the effort of clinging to the log.

His dreams, when he had drifted into a kind of sleep that was closer to confused wakefulness, arrived with violent flashbacks of the wave that may have covered the world, of his parents shouting at him for help from the top of their stone tower, and hellish visions of what might lurk below the cold, dark waters, what might be staring up at them with dead eyes.

Eventually, all sense of time and place slipped away until …

'Wha-? whoa!' Lief came to for a second time with a violent feeling of vertigo, like he was about to slip. Something heavy was on his leg that at least stopped him falling in the waters that still boiled and frothed too close for comfort.

It was Hell.

She pushed herself off him and scrambled back to her place at the other end of the broad trunk. Then she glared angrily at Lief, as if daring him to mention that during the long night she had crept down to where he lay. Lief thought about that for a moment and all it implied, then decided to file it away under *Yet more Things Hell Did That Made No Sense*.

For the tenth time in as many hours, bitter spit flooded into his throat and he leant forward and gagged, aware of Hell watching him with undisguised distaste – for her part, showing no sign of sickness … nor fear. Maybe she really didn't care? His head pounded and his whole body had cramped. He wondered if he'd ever feel well again. Hell had been right, the water hadn't gone in the night, but their home had, his parents … everything. Only the extreme likelihood of Hell's sneering stopped him from crying … that and the fact he was so thirsty, he didn't think he had enough water in his body left for tears. But his bottled-up grief made the sickness come flooding back and he gagged on a mucusy lump of bile, and spat. 'Urgh,' he groaned. 'I think I'm going to die.'

'No, you're not.'

'What makes you so sure?' Lief muttered. Hell looked at him intently.

'You've got things to do, Lief.' However, before he could ask what she meant by that, yet another wave of sickness hit him.

He retched, thin bile filling his mouth, then spat. Lief took a few deep breaths, before raising his head weakly to scan the horizon. He was not expecting to see anything – looking down just made him feel worse – but something caught his eye. Lief squinted.

Land!

The wave hadn't swept the world away! Maybe the water was going down, Hell was wrong, his parents would be fine if they'd clung to the tower. He felt shaky with relief, and they could get off this bloody log … and he'd be walking home. He unstuck his tongue from the roof of his mouth.

'Look!' Hell didn't look. 'I can see a hill! And it's coming up fast.' She still didn't look around, she was so …

A broad chalk cliff, ragged and partly new, thanks to the flood, could now be seen clearly. The morning sun rose like a sore eye in the east. It struck the white stone, turning it bloody, adding to the eeriness alongside the still-tumbling, still-angry clouds which fled like wrecks across the sky in the talons of a spiteful wind that shredded the waves.

They were close enough now that Lief could make out a narrow beach at the foot of the reddened cliffs. In just a few moments, hope had replaced despair. If you hold on long enough, your luck will change, thought Lief. And, at that moment, he made the decision that would steer his life: *He would hold on. And he would get back home.*

[BARD]
*A wind can whip,*
*From foul to fair.*
*As life can turn,*
*Upon a hair.*

Lief checked the current and saw that the way they were going, they would miss the relatively easy landing on the sand and hit rocks instead. He didn't understand water – at least not in this quantity – but he was fairly sure they could turn the tree trunk … he dipped his feet into the water and started moving a bit like he was on a horse.

'What in the gods' names are you doing?'

'We have to somehow turn this thing around, or we'll smash to pieces on those rocks, but I can't work out how!'

Lief heard a snapping noise, turned and saw that Hell had pulled off one of the brittle roots that jutted from the stump and was using it like a sort of lever in the water.

'I'm not sure that will work.' He turned back to concentrate on what he was doing but, even as hc said it, Lief noticed they had changed course a fraction. Each

23

stuck stubbornly to their own chosen
method and, by degrees, the front of the tree
swung around to point at the sandy part of
the shore.

> [BARD]
> *Two lost, not lost at all,*
> *Two fates unfeted.*
> *Beneath cracked tower and broken wall*
> *The Dragon watched. And waited.*

A few minutes later, they hit the beach hard;
the impact took Lief by surprise and he went
head over heels. Hell jumped lithely from
the trunk and strutted past Lief, who shook
sand out of his eyes and stared up at the wall
of reddened chalk that looked even more
sinister and unnatural close up. If he thought
he'd feel any better for being on dry land he
was about to be disappointed: the abnormal
light, the rushing water and the damaged
sky all made it feel like they were still living
in a feverish dream where he was trapped in
an alien landscape. With Hell. Was this what
the Other World was like: *Heðan*, where the
dead went? It did not feel like a place for
humans at all.

What now? he wondered.

The only consolation was that the water that had cut this shoreline since yesterday had exposed a freshwater spring in the rockface. Both children raced forward and drank for a very long time.

Eventually, his thirst quenched, Lief turned and surveyed the area around them.

The retreating sea had left a jumble of washed-up detritus discarded haphazardly across the sands. Lief made a short, panicked scan of the immediate area for *dead people* and breathed easier when he saw no tell-tale lumps of soggy clothes. Even at his age he'd seen enough death. Harsh winters would take the old and the very young without fail; raiders would sometimes come and they would need to be killed. But the sight of a corpse still gave him the shivers.

If the body was not bloated with plague or hacked to pieces, the dead would be prepared for burial by the druid, Kan, who had arranged their faces in death to make them look alive – often a lot healthier, in fact, than the last few months they had been sick.

Kan had died just the previous winter and, with no druid to prepare him, the wives had done their best, but within days his face had gone an unpleasant green and a quick decision to burn him was made.

Lief wondered if you would go to *Heban* if you hadn't had a proper burial, even if you had been a druid. He supposed you did, but where was the proof? Unlike Hell, Lief had no wish to talk to the dead, but it would have been reassuring to know they went there for sure – perhaps if …

'Would you stop bloody daydreaming and help me with this!' Hell was struggling with something stuck under a pile of broken branches.

[BARD]
*Quick the word,*
*And bright the blade.*
*Both can cut:*
*For boy or maid.*

'The sword's mine!' said Lief, but without much conviction. It was a huge tarnished lump and he had the distinct impression it would make him look ridiculous.

'I found it,' said Hell simply.

'I didn't think swords were your thing – you're more into spells and potions … you know, basically *pretending*.' Hell shot him a withering glare through her messy fringe. 'Hey, where are you going?' He started to jog after her.

'Up there,' she said. 'Whilst you had your head in the sand, I saw a settlement through the trees, it's part of a building seems like.' She looked unsure of herself. 'Anyway, there could be people.'

'Great, they could lend us a boat or we could stay with them until the water goes and we'll go back.'

'Go back where, Lief the Lesser? There's no *there* anymore, in case you haven't noticed, it's all covered by water.'

'The water's disappearing, my parents will be worried sick, your brother …'

'If you knew him like I do, you wouldn't be in such a hurry to go back.'

'OK, then my parents …'

'You can run back if you like.'

'Yes, I will. They're my family.'

'They're all dead,' said Hell harshly. In spite of his weakness, Lief felt his anger rising.

'You might think that, I reckon you wish they were.' And as soon as the words came out, it occurred to Lief he could easily imagine why.

Their settlement had abandoned them when they had been orphaned. "The weak aren't meant to live long." His father had muttered over his ale. Lief remembered being angry. "But you have to help them …

we all have to stick together, that's the best way to survive." His father looked up in surprise – Lief was always quiet. Unusually small for his age and placid, most people in the village had decided long ago that Lief was nice enough but he would never amount to anything. Hence his nickname.

Lief thought his father would be angry at his outburst. Instead – if anything – he'd looked proud. In the end, Lief's mother had seen to it that Hell and her brother did not starve those first few winters before they could fend for themselves.

He was obviously glad but he couldn't help wishing it had been someone else on the log … his parents.

He stared at Hell in silence but her face was unreadable. 'You're wrong about everybody being dead. I'm going to find them,' he said eventually.

'And I'm going to find out what caused this and actually do something about it,' said Hell.

'What? Another spell that doesn't exist, more made up magic? … there might be a broomstick up there or some elves.'

'Look …' Hell spun round, sword in hand.

'Whoa, careful where you point the pointy end of that thing,'

'… you don't have to come, you can stay on this beach and daydream until someone rescues you. I'm going to discover what this place is all about.'

'Well, that might give you a clue.' Lief pointed at the near horizon and Hell followed his finger.

[BARD]
*A gruesome ship, tossed on high,*
*Betwixt graceless sea and deadly sky.*

Bile rushed back into his throat and the water he'd just drunk threatened to come up again. But why? It was just a boat.

'Who's sailing that thing? There's something dangerous about it.' Lief spoke for himself, but he could see that even Hell looked worried.

'There's wickedness lurking on that thing,' she murmured. It was true, the ship sliced through the water like a knife through flesh … but there was something else, there was something on board they could not see but Lief knew it was a threat. Worse than that, he felt terrified.

'That settlement you spoke about.' They needed to get off the beach, thought Lief. Right now. 'We can shelter up there.'

## Chapter 3: Ruins

After a few dead ends, they eventually made it to the ragged lip that marked the cliff edge along an overgrown path. His sickness beginning to fade, Lief was feeling light-headed with hunger, but he forgot about that as he straightened up and stared at the stronghold that lay before them.

'I've never seen anything so big.' It was huge – ten times larger than the largest tower enclosure he had seen – like a group of keeps, connected by walls. Except it was obviously deserted. Two of the towers had crumbled to little more than cones of rubble and the remaining walls were festooned with ivy, small shrubs and very green moss. 'There's no-one here,' he remarked. Hell stepped forward.

'Beware!' She said. 'Spirits live on in places such as this: ghouls who feed off the energy of the people that stray into their territory ... they'll steal your shadow and make an evil servant from it.' Standing behind her, Lief rolled his eyes.

'Let's go in and check it out – as you say, there might be a ghost or two, then again there might be something we actually need – like food or a well with fresh water,' he said, moving past her towards the first stone archway.

[BARD]

*A frigid wind will murmur, "Fate.".*
*Dry leaves attend the Marshward Gate,*
*Which drongs and sounds a mournful tune,*
*As shadows rearrange the gloom.*
*And down and down the echoes groan*
*through the rock and under stone.*

*So all alone, so all alone,*
*The Darkling Tower lies overgrown.*
*Awash, awash the Careful Court*
*with lichen, larks and Dragonwort.*
*Who skive, dive and trilly sing,*
*"Awake, awake! The one true King."*
*And deep beneath the battered skies,*
*The King he stirs to hear the cries …*

'Ahhh! It's the Undead! Stand back or I will smite you, foul creature!'

Something dry and husky that had once – a very long time ago – been human stared at them from a stone chair. Lief forced himself to approach.

'No, Hell, it's a *Mummy*,'

'Are you sure? It's got a …'

'Yes, quite sure,' said Lief quickly, 'I've heard about these, they prepare their

32

dead in some places and they use tricks to keep the flesh from rotting. But, you're right – they ought to have given him pants. He's got a crown on after all.'

'No, it must be very old, that's all,' murmured Hell, who had regained her composure, 'all his clothes have rotted away. Gold never rusts or rots.'

'Kings do.'

'Hmm.' Hell moved towards the mummified remains. Lief could see she meant to take the crown.

'Don't do that.'

'Do what?'

'Take the crown. It doesn't belong to us, Hell. Anyway, we need food and water. You can't eat gold.'

'You can use it to trade.'

'With who?' Hell shrugged. 'Look,' Lief went on, 'it's still not ours – and anyway, you're not meant to steal from the dead. It's bad luck.'

'It's bad luck not to take what you need when you need it, that's what my brother and I always say.' Lief saw that, as usual, she wasn't going to listen to him (or anyone). Hell went to snatch the crown but Lief darted forward, grabbing it from the gruesome head. Hell made a lunge for it too, but she didn't want to let go of the sword and with only one hand free, she gave Lief the advantage and he yanked with both hands. Hell lost her grip and Lief fell backwards holding the crown.

'Right!' said Hell through clenched teeth, looking furious. She brought the sword up, but Lief was too quick, flitting to higher ground with a grin. It had to be the first time in his life he'd got the better of Hell and he felt a flash of triumph. Just to annoy her, he popped the crown on his head.

So simple. So important.

> [BARD]
> *Sparkle light,*
> *But who can bear her?*
> *The crown sits heavy,*
> *For the wearer.*

A flash of blue-white light cut through his skull like a very cold dagger. In an instant he saw the ruins around him from long before, when they were whole …
… and there was something else he couldn't quite see, rather he sensed: it lay hidden, very deep, but Lief *knew* it was something colossal – and it slept in the heart of the hill. He felt its power and its menace.

> [BARD]
> *Through the rock and under stone,*

*The dragon sleeps alone, alone …*

And this was why he missed what came next.

For when the vision faded, and Lief opened his eyes, it was quite a different scene to the one he'd been half-expecting (Hell beating him senseless with that huge rusty sword of hers).

Her habitual angry glaring was directed in another direction, which would have been a relief, were it not for the fact that from being alone in this place, Lief and Hell were suddenly – and completely – surrounded.

Lief's first observation was that the people encircling them were all children (five largish, dozens small: all staring) and, secondly, they had a cauldron, which didn't fill Lief with happy thoughts that things were going to turn out well. He'd heard enough gory tales of other, more basic-brutal tribes to seriously worry that they could end up as part of someone's next meal.

The other very noticeable thing about them was they seemed wholly unaware of – or unconcerned by – Hell, who was still snarling like a stray cat and waving a weapon under their noses. Instead, they were staring at Lief.

At the top of his head, to be precise.

'I don't think you need that thing,' Lief said to Hell out the side of his mouth. He had a pretty good idea what had caught their attention. 'They're not dangerous.' Hell shot him an *are you kidding?* look but lowered her sword a fraction anyway.

A large boy with a flat, expressionless face stepped awkwardly towards Lief. Both newcomers could immediately see why he moved badly: the bottom half of his left leg was missing – whether by accident or by birth, Lief couldn't tell either way. The boy had a tightly-bound tree branch where his leg should have been: it seemed sturdy enough, but crooked.

'Who are you?' the boy asked. He had a strange sing-song way of making the words but spoke the same language – Uralic – as Lief did.

'Ask them how he can wear the sacred crown without his brain boiling and his eyes popping out of his head,' a girl about a year younger than Lief said, and came forward, immediately followed by another girl with the same vivid red hair. They were twins: the one who spoke, grinning through crooked teeth, the other, silent and watchful.

'… and his ears exploding.' A lot of the little ones, half in shadow, giggled at the bony, dark-haired girl who said this. Her accent was thick, it was almost as if she had a heavy cold. Lief, whose eyes were blue, had never seen anyone with black eyes before. He stared at her until the skinny girl looked unsure of herself and took a step back. It was odd, but they seemed almost as afraid of him as they were curious. It had to be the crown.

Lief took it off.

'Ahhhh!' they all cried, as if he'd just put his hands in molten metal.

'He *is* the King!' breathed the huge boy with the missing leg and all the little ones took up a chant,

'… the King, the King, the King, yaay!'

'What's a king?' one of them asked.

'Shhh,' said all the others, looking fearful again.

'No he's not!' Someone near the back came forward. Out of all the others, the boy was most like Lief: blond with blue eyes and similar clothing. He could have come from Doggerland and Lief was ridiculously pleased to see him: he smiled, but the boy glared back.

'Don't *say* that, Etta,' the frizzy, red-haired girl pointed a dirty finger at Hell, she frowned '… she could maybe chop off our heads.'

For the first time in months, Hell smiled.

'I'm not a king,' Lief thought he should put a stop to that before things got out of hand.

'See,' the boy, Etta, said. He looked at Lief less aggressively but kept his distance. I wonder why, thought Lief.

'Yes he is, otherwise he couldn't have taken the crown and worn it,' the large boy with the wooden leg spoke again. 'We've been up here for seven days and none of us has been able to touch it without burning ourselves. Look.' He showed Lief his own huge hand with an angry red welt across it. He looked like the type who made up his mind, and then rarely changed it.

'Nolly's right,' said the frizzy girl, her chin jutting forward. She knew her own mind, too – she was strong-headed in a different way from the large boy: more like fire to his rock. But she could be persuaded. 'Then again, perhaps he just doesn't know it yet?' The girl grinned cheekily at him and Lief saw the ghost of a ghost of a smile on her sister's face. 'I'm Kran, by the way. This here stronghold is called Vantage. So, where are youz from, Your Royally Highnesses?'

Hell shot Lief a glance that said, *'Don't tell them anything.'* She had a look on her face Lief had seen a hundred times. Two hundred. It meant she was up to something. She turned to the newcomers and threw them her most haughty look. Here it comes, thought Lief. 'I am Hell, Warrior Witch!' she cried in a loud voice and they all took a step back. 'And he,' – she pointed dramatically at Lief who thought to himself *oh no*, – 'is indeed a prince from our realm.'

'So where is that?' asked the blond boy, Etta – the only one not overawed.

'The Kingdom of Silence.'

'Oooh,' the Little Ones said.

*'The land of grass that floats below the waves,'* chanted Hell, who was becoming quite the performer recently. *'And those who go are the bravest of braves!'*

'How do you get there?' The Little Ones knew a half-decent story when they heard it.

*'On a drunken boat – or a sunken goat!'*

'Let's go now!' The Little Ones began to jump up and down.

*'To enter the land of sunken seas, you have to ask the bumble bees.'*

'But we don't know how!' wailed the Little Ones. Lief noticed that even the bigger ones were smiling now. Except Etta.

'*Well, if you don't know how, then ask a cow.*'

'But we've never met any of them!'

'They just *moo*, anyway.'

'Cows like bumble bees, I've seen them together.'

'Shut up, stupid.'

'Be silent!' commanded Hell, turning scary, like a strict adult. The Little Ones fell quiet … then Hell gave them a secret wink. For someone who was so miserable most of the time, she was pretty good with kids, thought Lief.  She continued.

[HELL]
*Only seagulls know*
*where the cold winds go.*
*And only the whales*
*love the Golden Shales -*

*For on the silent sea bed,*
*Lies the Kingdom that Fled.*

Hell finished to an awed hush and turned to them. 'Why have you got that cauldron?'

'We found it! We found it!' yelled the Little Ones (totally unfazed by Hell's song).

'Yep, we were going to use it to cook,' said red-headed Kran.

'And have baths!' they all shouted.

'And hide in it … from the Gauts,' said the very littlest. Ever so quietly.

There was dead silence.

'*Gauts?*' said Hell.

## Chapter 4: Gauts

[GAUTS]
*we so bad make zombies look sick*
                              *put us down n' we'll cut*
                    *you quick*
*take what we want ain't no 1 stoppin' us*
                                   *'cos we're boss*
*not to be crossed tossed on seas*
                         *we come at you*
                         *you bend your knee*
                    *you've got no choice we're*
                              *the voice*
                                        *the sword*
                                        *the last word*
*your final breath*

        *We are death.*

'The Gauts have taken over the marsh, on the other side of this hill,' Kran was saying. 'They like it cold, and they don't like to stray too far from that precious ship of theirs. Also, they're not human – they cover their faces most of the time but they have huge mouths with tusks or some have teeth like a dead shark and eyes that glow yellow in the dark. And they want land, they always want land – especially now, when it's disappearing – and they're here to hunt us, take us back, cos' we all escaped. 'Cept the Little Ones – they're refugees from the villages on the coast the Gauts destroyed. We found them wandering about, they don't take 'em if they're too young to work.'

'Hunt you?' asked Lief.

'Yes, they're taking slaves, some to work for them here, others to take back to their country beyond the farthest sea, where my grandpa says it's all ice and volcanoes. They stole us from all over the place: Nolly's from so far North the sun never shines and Nuria's from right at the bottom of the world where it never stops, but …' Kran frowned. 'Recently, the Gauts, they've been acting strange. That ship of theirs is weird, too, it moans at night.'

'We saw a ship when we arrived, after the flood,' said Hell quietly. 'Where are we?'

'This is Albion … and the Gauts are trying to capture it, just like everywhere else, but they're taking their time, something is making them cautious.'

'They're scared of coming up here,' said the large boy, 'they stomp about at the foot of the hill but avoid the slopes and the beach behind. Kran's right, there's something about them lately, the land about them is dying, they're … wrong.' And as soon as he said it, Lief thought about the mad traveller back home and shivered. The traveller had used that word, too. He had been talking about Gauts, too – Lief was sure. But he called them something different – Trollhaten Beasts.

' … summert rattles them about this hill … but they won't leave it to go inland and conquer – I think there's something important up here that they want, not just us.' Kran seemed the most talkative, and her sister didn't say a thing.

'The Gauts need to find something that will stop all the land they capture from dying,' the small, dark girl, Nuria, spoke with quiet certainty. 'The village elders said that they will burn every village and kill everyone to find it.'

'Gauts kill everything,' agreed Nolly.

'Well, they won't come up here and they won't leave: but they'll still be wanting us back sure enough – that's why it's a fine thing you came along – turns the tables, evens the odds, *settles the scores*.'

'I'm not …' Lief started to say again.

'Do you camp in these ruins?' Hell interrupted him.

'No,' said a lot of the Little Ones, 'it's a secret.'

'We move about,' Etta's expression dared them to ask more.

'We usually sleep in the woods outside the castle, might be ghosts here, until you came along …' Kran's voice trickled away as she saw the expression on Etta's face. 'What?'

'Urgh!' Etta sort of grunted and glared.

'What's that supposed to mean?'

'Nnn, maa ngggg.'

'Have you been eating those funny berries, Etta?'

'… we don't know them,' he pointed with his eyes at Lief and Hell.

'Sure we know them!' Kran said brightly. 'He's a king and she's a scary warrior-whatchamacallit-sing-a-song(-or-two).'

'He's no king.'

45

'That's right, I never said ...'
Something worrying had just occurred to Lief: if they made him their leader, he would have to stay.

'Sure he's a king, are you blind? Ain't you seen that big sparkly thing on top of his head there? And they marched into the holy place cool as you like and met the old king who gave him that and they're not turned into blotchy toads or worse ... *and* that means they can definitely be trusted. And we'll be safe. Sorted.'

'Yes,' said Lief before anyone else said anything and especially before Hell started to sing again. He'd just reached a decision: they should remain – for now, at least – up here on this mound with cover of trees and a few remains of walls: whether he was a king or not. It was the best spot for miles around for seeing what was coming ... and whilst he didn't like the idea of the Gauts, they had a ship.

And if he was to go back, a ship was something Lief wanted right now. Very much indeed.

'We are better off here for the time being,' he said in what he hoped was a kingly way.

'Seriously, why did you tell them I was a king? Those Gauts don't sound pleasant. In the least. And we don't need a new tribe – we've got one, and the first chance I get, I'm going back to find them. This babysitting you've got us into is temporary.'

Hell and Lief had moved away from the others. The sun had moved past midday and most of them had found hollows in which to curl up and nap. Nuria had explained in her thick accent that they usually slept during the day and moved at night, when it was harder to be spotted by any Gaut search parties.

'Well, you are the son of a chief, that's practically the same.'

'One that you think is useless and you think I'm an idiot.'

'I never said that,' replied Hell seriously, 'I just think you could be … *better*.

She gave him one of her looks. 'Time for you to prove everyone wrong, Lief the Lesser.'

'What?' Lief had no idea what Hell was talking about most of the time – especially these days. '…Whatever … anyway, more importantly, what's all this stuff about being a warrior witch?'

The corner of Hell's mouth twitched.

'It sounded good at the time – anyway it's good if they're in awe of you and a little scared of me.'

'Except the Little Ones, they seem to think you're their new big sister.' Hell looked like she was remembering something unpleasant.

'Well, I know what it's like to be them, I guess,' she said. Lief took a deep breath.

'How long do you think you can keep this up?'

'What up?'

'You know what I mean, sooner or later they're going to figure out that you're no more magic than they are and I'm not royal-born.' Hell rolled her eyes as if Lief was the stupidest person she knew.

'Wrong question!'

'OK, so what is the right question?'

'Well, how come you were able to take that crown and how come these Gauts won't come up here?'

'Because it's just a lump of shiny metal.' It was Lief's turn to talk as if speaking to a moron. 'And because we're on a hill: warriors don't like climbing hills, especially with thick trees.'

'I'm not so sure. It's one thing a bunch of kids thinking this place is sacred, but those Gauts seem stranger and stronger than anything you've seen in your life. I think they could storm this hill anytime they like, but something's stopping them and that's got to be magic. And that's my speciality – the wave, those Gauts, I … *we* could fix all that. Meeting these kids is just what we need.'

Lief couldn't believe what he was hearing. He opened his mouth to disagree when they heard a stick snap behind them.

'I knew you were lying.'

They turned and saw the boy, Etta. Lief had no idea how long he'd been standing behind them, or how much he had heard but, judging by the expression on his face, he'd heard a lot. Enough, anyway.

'I knew you weren't a king, you're just like me, we probably come from the same place, and you …' he stared at Hell who met his gaze steadily, so eventually Etta lowered his eyes, '… I don't know what you are,' he mumbled.

'Are you going to tell the others?' Part of Lief hoped he would.

Etta didn't say anything for a while. He looked down the hill, at where the marshes lay: a hazy strip of flatlands. This was where their real enemy was – Lief thought so anyway, but he was fast coming to the conclusion that everyone's priorities were different.

'I don't trust you and I'll be watching you,' Etta said, 'but I won't tell the others – not for now, at least. King or not, we need a leader who hasn't been captured by the Gauts: you might have the gods on your side and you're wearing a crown ...' he shrugged, 'you don't look much, but who knows?'

## Chapter 5: Vantage

At first Lief couldn't sleep. Judging by the restless movements around him, the others were also on edge and alert. All of them had had hard lives: they had seen more than children should see, and had suffered. But the plague, the Gauts and now the wave had eclipsed everything terrible that had gone before. Sleep slunk about the fringes of their camp like a cat keeping its distance. The darkness settled on them like a heavy fog and, in the silence, their troubled thoughts clamoured for attention.

But, finally, the Little Ones began to settle.

Lief was not surprised. He remembered a time he was small, when he did not dwell on hurts, when his mind was quick to say, *get over, get past and move on. Play and laugh and I'll feel better.*

By and by, the silent sense of safety in the old castle seeped into all their tired bones and bodies and each child slept. Even Lief.

The night passed and the morning came … and with it came the light, as it always will.

[BARD]

*The sun shimmered – shyly at first,*
*Peeking through the reeds and marshes,*
*Pinking pools of water,*
*That splashed up paths, then passes.*

*To where the ancients lay,*
*To Vantage – upon higher ground –*
*slumbered silence that whispered,*
*'Safe, sacred here, and sound.'*

*The sun, ere long escaped the mire,*
*burned brightly and the crane birds lifted.*
*Skimming across the shallow waters,*
*As cushion clouds drifted.*

*Traversing now a new horizon, piloting*
*inland, up the soft folds of vale,*
*As Albion awoke once more,*
*From old woodland, down, to dale.*

Lief lifted his head drowsily and looked out
on the green folds of countryside that
unfurled into the distance. This new land
was certainly beautiful. Where he lay, Lief
was warm and comfortable, and it was nice
to look at something other than waves. He
thought about getting up, but the others
were still fast asleep and clinging to the log
had exhausted him. He drifted off again.

Later, the morning sun that had promised a fine day had turned into clouds, then more clouds, then chilly rain that annoyed Lief to wakefulness.

He emerged from the hollow where he'd been sleeping to see Hell prodding a damp fire with the rusty sword. There were no flames to the fire, just a lot of smoke.

'We need decent shelter, Your Royal Bloody Highness,' she muttered.

Lief ignored her. Anyway, she was wrong, he thought as he wrapped his arms around his thin chest and tried not to shiver; what they needed first was proper food. From midday to dusk the previous day, he'd watched their new companions harvesting early autumn berries from bushes, looking for edible lizards and chewing grubs. Hell might have approved, but Lief knew that hot food and full bellies kept people happy. Happy meant they listened: listened meant they worked together, and that was their only chance if they were going to survive. And escape. Sooner or later, these Gauts would be coming for them – conquerors (human or not) always wanted their prize, that much Lief was sure of. They wanted land and they wanted slaves and both were on their doorstep. Their ship was everybody's best chance, Lief told himself.

[BARD]
*King be brave?*
*Or king be clever?*
*Lord or knave?*
*It was now or never.*


Lief looked around at the cold, wet children. He didn't know anything about being a leader. He suspected Hell said he was a prince mainly to annoy him, and Etta would probably be happy if he failed.

Lief looked down at the crown held limply in his hand. It was a cold, dead thing, but when he placed it on his head he felt another flash of memory trying to barge into his normal, everyday thoughts.

[BARD]
*Swords sing,*
*A fiery sky.*
*Twice ragged wing,*
*One slitted eye.*


Now is not the time (he told himself). *Focus.*

The visions – no more than just blurred images – of men and monsters, armour and scale faded and he opened his eyes. In the meantime, everyone had stopped what they were doing and was looking at him strangely, which was hardly a surprise. He took a deep breath; he just had to go for it.

'Hi.' Gods, no, that sounded terrible. He still had their attention but in a few seconds he'd lose them. Perhaps forever.

'Listen!' That came out louder than he wanted – but it did the trick. Nolly's back straightened and, out of the corner of his eye, he even saw Hell stop poking at the fire and look up from underneath her black fringe.

'You do not know me, we come from different places – all of us – we have different stories, different hopes and even our futures may be different. But, for now, we're together …' No, that just sounded like he didn't want to be there … *c'mon Lief*, he thought, *I can do better than this* '… and yet! We're more alike than we know,' he saw a faint nod from Kran and that gave him the confidence to stop shouting, '… much more,' he added in a murmur and, to Lief's satisfaction, most of the children leaned forward to catch what he was saying.

Words are like magic – proper magic – he thought: you can shape them, to bend people. 'You've chosen me to lead you and …' He'd been on the point of saying something like *I'll do my best*, or *I hope I do a good job*, but that's not what they wanted from him - they wanted a rock. '… And so I shall. This new day,' he looked up at the sky and smiled ruefully, 'has not started well, but a new day it is and new hope. From today we leave the past behind. No more, I say! No more skulking in the shadows by day, tiptoeing in terror at night, no more eating cold grubs and berries! No more cold, no more hunger, no more fear and no more Gauts! We are small and we are few, but we start to fight back from this day, this day of days.' And Lief saw that they had all risen to their feet, even the Little Ones were quiet and nodding. 'This is our time!'

Lief stopped. It was just a start, but it was OK.

He glanced at Hell, expecting mockery, but was surprised to see her looking pleased with herself.

'So what do we need do?' asked Kran. After Lief's pep talk, the rain had petered out, they had got the fire going properly and now everyone was drying in the pale sun.

'First of all, we need proper food – fighting food … we need meat,' replied Lief.

'And how do we get that? We've got no bows … and none of us knows anything about hunting.' Ha! Thought Lief, she's not going to like this, but she asked for it.

'I know someone who does,' he said, turning and smiling at Hell who scowled back. For a moment he thought Hell would ignore the invitation, but she was a good hunter thanks to all her older brother had taught her, and he was counting on the fact she knew that now was the time to show team spirit. He'd forgotten about her new and unlikely role of children's entertainer.

Hell stood slowly and winked at the Little Ones, who sensed something for their benefit was in the pipeline.

[HELL]
*'It's quite absurd, to catch a bird*
*without a bow and arrow.*
*It can't be done – it won't be fun!'*

'You'll think of a way,' said Lief, refusing to be drawn into the song.

*'Well, I have heard, to get your bird*
*you pinch salt upon its tail.*
*It's no use with the Flubby Goose*
*But works with the Kuku Quail.'*

'Go for it,' said Lief, hoping she'd stop soon.

*The Palpanese of the Soggy Seas,*
*When they hear their tummies rumble,*
*Make magic spells from cockle shells,*
*And feast on seagull crumble.*

*I know the ways of crows and jays*
*(though larks remain a mystery).*
*Partridge, pigeon, I love too well*
*- Lyrebirds are ancient history.*

'Are you going, or not?'

*I shall, I will, fear not, King Clot,*
*I'll catch your birds with cunning words,*
*and we'll roast them in that pot!*

Her humour apparently back, Hell
grinned on-then-off and got up.

'Wait!' blurted out Nuria, jumping
up, then stopping, 'can I come?'

Hell turned and stared at her. Nuria
looked nervous of the older, taller girl but
stood her ground.

'OK,' said Hell curtly, 'just don't
blunder about scaring everything away.'
And, with that, she started down the hill so
Nuria had to trot to keep up. There was a
pause as the others watched them leave.

'Well, if they're going hunting for
things with feathers, it's scales and shells

we're after. C'mon, Fran,' Kran said, 'you and me, we're off fishing.'

After they had gone, Nolly ambled over, with a hesitant smile. Lief was keen for a closer look at the wooden stump he used for his left leg but, instead, he forced his eyes to meet Nolly's flat features and curiously angled eyes.

The large boy cleared his throat.

'I was born without it, so I don't know any different.'

'Oh.' Inwardly, Lief chided himself – he must have stared after all.

'Don't worry,' Nolly said in the concerned tones of someone who spends their life fretting about other people's feelings. 'Everyone is curious. And it looks a bit wonky right now, so I don't mind you laughing. The Gauts took my proper wooden leg to stop me running away, so I made this myself … from ash. It's not pretty, but I can work all day with it on. I'll make another one, when I've got time.' He rubbed his huge hands together. Lief saw calluses and prominent sinews – signs of manual labour. His fingers, on the other hand, were long and surprisingly agile. 'I'm not much of a talker … like your Hell (*my Hell?*, thought Lief) … but I make things and I wondered if you minded if I built us a shelter? For the

Little Ones, mainly,' he added quickly, 'but for us, too – keep the weather off when we're asleep. It won't be warm forever, we're not far enough south for that.'

'Of course,' said Lief. 'That would be brilliant. I'd be glad to help, if you show me what needs to be done.' Nolly's eyes widened: kings and princes – even chiefs of small settlements -didn't do this kind of work. Perhaps I'll be different, thought Lief. 'Just tell me if I'm getting in your way.'

'Well, there's a song you can sing to help remember how to build. There are lots of songs, really, to help you work, but this is the one I was taught by my father – he was a master builder in our village.' He looked apologetically at Lief. 'I know you don't like singing over much.' He said it in an almost childlike way and Lief couldn't help but smile.

'Of course not, sing anything you like. Just don't expect me to join in.'

'Ha, no, of course not,' Nolly blew his cheeks up and spluttered theatrically – as if to demonstrate that Nolly knew a joke when he heard one. Then he made a show of mastering his mirth. 'You're a king after all, you have to keep stern and proper.'

'Yes, Nolly,' Lief replied, 'I suppose I do.'

## [NOLLY]

*To build your house, clear the ground,*
*Pick your spot and make it sound.*

Nolly recited as he went about dragging
away debris from a flat piece of the
courtyard where he'd chosen to erect the
shelter. He had a slow way of working, but
everything – even how he uprooted nettles –
was so on-purpose, so necessary that Lief
(who was entirely unpractical) recognised a
natural craftsman right away.

> *Then set the size and dig o' drains,*
> *Make them well in case it rains.*

Etta came over and started to help. He had
a methodical way about him, too. Lief
watched and, not for the first time, reflected
that he would have liked to be friends with
this boy – but that didn't look likely.

> *Now set the walls with heavy stones,*
> *They bind the house, for they're its bones.*

The Little Ones came over – Etta scowled,
but Nolly didn't shoo them away. Lief saw

how gentle he was with them, even when they got under his feet. Foot.

'Why don't you help collect rocks for the walls,' Lief suggested to them and they all nodded: collecting rocks was easy, as stone from the walls and archways littered the castle courtyard. Lief went off to help, leaving the actual building to the experts.

*Then windows, door, a hole – for smoke:*
*Too big you'll freeze, too small you'll choke.*

In under an hour, the shelter was beginning to take shape. The walls went up easily as most of the stone they were using was square cut and Etta seemed to have a knack for locking them together.

'I saw some clay banks further down towards the beach, we can seal the cracks with that – it'll also dry hard enough and help bind them.' Lief could see Nolly was pleased with what he'd done so far. He was red-faced and his thick hair was clumped with sweat but it was amazing how his wooden leg hardly seemed to trouble him.

'It looks fantastic; we'll be warm and dry thanks to you.'

*Build it well and build it true,*
*And these walls will bind with you,*

*Henceforth, wherever you may roam,*
*You will always have a home.*

Said Nolly to no-one in particular.

By lunchtime, they had made good progress
gathering material for the roof: young ash
trees were bent and uprooted for
crossbeams, the slimmer branches woven
with thick grass to make panels.

They had just started to lay the
panels on top of the crossbeams, where Etta
was using nettle stalks to lash them together,
when Hell arrived with Nuria.

They were out of breath. 'There
were Gauts!' Nuria blurted out, 'they saw us
and we ran and they ran, they were roaring
at us … but they stopped at the hill.'

Nuria was terrified and Hell had red
spots on her normally white-as-milk
complexion, but her expression was
unreadable.

'Did you see anything else?' Lief
asked Hell.

'No, and it's not right,' Nuria was
too agitated to keep quiet, 'there are trees to
shclter, water for drinking and berries to eat
and there's even those holes where creatures
live … but no animals. Even the birds are
gone. Just flown away. Before we nearly

stumbled into the Gauts we saw nothing …
it's so quiet in the woods. Like a dead place.'

'It's *Them*,' said Hell flatly, in that
sure-seeming way of hers, then looked
around to see if anyone disagreed with her.
'Even the animals are fleeing. These Gauts
are worse than the wave, worse than the
plague.'

'Where did they go when they
turned back? Were they really afraid of
coming up the hill? Lief was keen to find out
more – anything they knew about the Gauts
was useful. But there was something else: at
just the mention of their name, the crown
had tightened on his head, as if it were
tensing. He focused on Nuria, instead, to
ward off any more visions. Right now he
needed facts, not the fantasies the crown
served up.

'They went back towards their
camp,' said Nuria, whose breathing had
evened out by now. 'One thing,' she glanced
at Hell, perhaps for confirmation she should
continue. Hell nodded imperceptibly. 'The
ship has gone.'

Everyone looked at each other.

'Fran and Kran are down by the
beach!' Nolly blurted out what everyone had
instantly thought. Lief turned to run down
the path to warn them. But he didn't need
to. Lief saw bright red hair before Fran's

grinning face was visible through the undergrowth crowding the path. He hardly knew her, but relief ran through him.

The twins had heard what they were talking about, and told them, 'The ship's not tied up because it's zipping back and forth along the coast. They can't land on the beach, cos' of the magic, but they'll not let up watching us - you can be sure of that.' Fran and Kran had taken off their shawls and were using them as sacks. 'Didn't stop us collecting all these beauties,' Kran added, flinging open the sack and winking at the Little Ones.

Lief looked at the haul of mussel shells, oysters and baby crabs with alarm. *How could any of that be edible?* he thought. However, only Etta and Hell seemed as doubtful as he did; the rest of them - especially Nuria, who was also from a place by the sea – looked delighted. Lief relaxed; it looked like they would eat well, tonight. But they would have to be careful now about leaving Vantage.

[BARD]
*E'en as they made Vantage new,*
*Watched by Gauts through jaundice eyes,*
*They were young and they were few,*
*And fortunes fall as well as rise.*

65

After Fran and Kran's return, Lief had left the relative safety of the walls to watch the Gaut's camp from the cover of tree trunks and meshed undergrowth. The ship was back, he saw. There was something about the way the Gauts moved about that suggested they did not like the sun. It was mid-afternoon and still very warm, so most went to lie in the shadows thrown out by their ship or remained in their shelters. When they did venture into the sunlight, they did so quickly, crossing from one shaded area to another with huge strides. They are nocturnal creatures, Lief decided. They would need watching by night.

They walked as if they wanted to crush the ground beneath them. Even at this distance their heads were huge and misshapen – like giant, brutally-made versions of real humans. Lief thought of the stories of the far North where the Earth bled its boiling insides onto ice that lay in thick sheets and the sun never shone.

This inhuman place was their home and the crucible that made their mettle and moulded their bones.

He shivered in the warm afternoon light.

Lief stayed for a long while, wondering how to defeat them. Eventually, he turned and climbed up the hill, back to the reassuring walls of Vantage, just in time to see Etta and Nolly emerge from the undergrowth rolling a large stone slab between them. It threatened to topple at any moment, crushing someone's legs or arms. Lief ran forward to help, then immediately realised he was just getting in the way. He stepped away.

'What is it?' he asked to cover his embarrassment. Etta ignored the question, but Nolly was ready with an answer.

'It's some sort of table, I think,' he braced his good leg and heaved.

'But it's round?' said Lief.

'Never thought about it before,' Nolly was straining, 'but now I do, it's better than square, more people can eat at it.'

'... and everyone is the same,' Lief finished. He liked that. Lief wasn't sure what happened in other settlements but, in theirs, the headman always sat in the middle surrounded by the elders and his warriors, then the women, then the children at the edges, furthest from the fire … and the best food.

When he got back home, he would build a table like this, he decided.

He placed himself directly behind the table and helped push. On one side, the stone was perfectly smooth and pleasantly cool. What Lief imagined to be the underside was rough and covered in earth and clogged debris from where it had lain for years, obscured by bramble.

'Tomorrow we must clear the rest of these briars and thorn bushes away,' he said, and Nolly nodded, as if taking orders from Lief was the most natural thing in the world.

That'll put Hell's ancient sword to some use, he thought.


Getting the table into place took far longer than they had imagined. It had taken ages to find three boulders that were roughly the same size to act as supports, and by the time they had manoeuvred it into place, their knuckles were bleeding and the skin on Lief's hands felt stripped.

He was tired, but most of all, he was ravenous.

This was just as well. Whilst they had been heaving and lugging, Fran and Kran had been opening the shells and scraping the contents into the cauldron that they had dug a small pit for, with a cavity beneath to light a fire. The little ones had helped carry water from a small stream they had found between the rocks; Nuria had showed them how to make a pail with sticks bent together to make a bucket shape, which was then lined with mud and bark to hold water.

Hell watched them working for a bit. Then she shrugged and disappeared into the woods on her own.

Lief thought it was her way of avoiding work, but she came back a while later with wild garlic, which she handed to Fran without a word, along with something stubby and white resembling a gnarled finger.

'See these,' she said to the small crowd of Little Ones who seemed to crowd around her wherever she went, 'they grow in the sunny spots along the trees. The bit that grows out of the ground looks like this:' she held up some dark green crinkly sprouts. 'You have to go and collect as many as you can find, and come back before it gets dark.'

The Little Ones ran off looking serious and important. Lief doubted they'd be much help, but it kept them busy.

And that's another trick to leadership, he thought to himself: keep people busy. He caught Hell's eye as she looked after them and, if he didn't know better, he'd say she almost smiled at him – and then he almost smiled back. But she turned and the moment was over. He studied her profile for a few moments longer; the half-smile had changed her face … very briefly she had looked … *nice*?

The broth in the cauldron started to simmer and it smelled OK. Considering it was made of things that looked to Lief entirely inedible, stone-like and, frankly, smelly. Lief scanned the hills beyond the marsh where the sun was going down, throwing out graded bands of red, turquoise and silver – like ripples in a pond - that washed the land beneath in a type of light he'd never known.

Lief paused to take it all in. It wasn't home, but there was no doubt about it, this new country had its witching hours: times of the day when the natural beauty gave way to something deeper, a sort of potency in the very sinew of the landscape, a power that disagreed with its outward gentleness. In just a short space of time, it felt to Lief that literally anything was possible here, in this place.

Or perhaps he should stop being so fanciful, he told himself – he was getting worse than Hell.

But then the crown flashed against his forehead and the coming night spoke to him …


[BARD]
*Under dark and crushing sky,*
*Something stirs that would be woken.*

'Stop daydreaming again!' Hell had come over.

Lief stared about. At the trees, where the voice seemed to be coming from.

*Flittered, flickered, slittered eye,*
*- Now speak the words as once were spoken!*

He blinked. Everyone was peering at him. Had they heard it too? These voices had to stop, but Lief had a feeling they were, if anything, going to get worse before they got any better. It was the crown. It felt tight around his head and hot. He would take it off, but …

'It's the first feast this castle must have seen in hundreds of years.' Kran obviously didn't feel comfortable during even quite short silences. 'Big occasion I'd say.'

'You should sit first,' Nolly gestured towards the circular table and smiled timidly at Lief.

But Lief did not sit. Something was happening … he could sense the land waking. It was like the day their home had been swept away: a kind of pressure that built in his head, behind the eyes, yet the force came from the earth, or the sky, or the rocks, or *everything* …

'Lief!'

'Hold!' his tone surprised Hell and her mouth snapped shut.

And then the voice came again, rushing at him through the dark trees, out of the cracks in the old stone walls, from the sky itself.

> [BARD]
> *Far too long this land has lain,*
> *Crushed between Trollhaten jaws,*
> *But the dragon sleeps unslain,*
> *See its scales, feel its claws.*
>
> *Lief the Lesser summon Seven,*
> *For something stirs that would be woken.*
> *Betwixt Netherworld, and in Heaven:*
> *Speak the words as they were spoken!*

Finally, by degrees, his head cleared and the crown cooled. He had no time to wonder what words the voice had been talking about and why he should speak them – something else was happening.

'Look,' he said, ignoring the alarmed stares still directed at him. He pointed at the cauldron – although he didn't really have to. The noises it was making would attract quite enough attention to itself on their own.

'Gods!' Kran going over and peering in. 'Look at that great big pot of ours – it's filling up!'

Everyone looked, even Hell. And it wasn't just the noises. Lief found himself teased forward, drawn by his nose and his rumbling stomach to the rich, stewy aromas that floated about the clearing.

He looked in.

To be fair to them, Fran and Kran had done a good job, but this was something else.

Somehow, the cauldron was now filled with several different types of meat; also wild onions and plump barley and it was all bobbing about in a bubbling, creamy broth.

'How has this happened?' Nolly was curious, but the others didn't seem to care, they were just delighted.

'It's a magic cauldron – *obviously* …
and that's the most delicious food I've
smelled in my whole flippin' life!' Kran was
practically jumping up and down on the
spot. 'Just imagine what it's actually like in
your belly.'

'There's venison in there,' said Etta
who was smiling, 'I haven't tasted that for
over a year.'

'And crispy pork, like my mother
made!' Nolly looked close to tears of pure
joy.

'Cracked peas.'

'Crab claws!'

'Chicken!'

'… and cabbage! What? I like
cabbage.' Nolly had the look of someone
who probably liked most things, Lief thought
to himself.

'Did you make the cauldron do this?'
Kran looked at Hell. There was a pause,
whilst Hell rearranged her features into the
most haughty and mysterious look she could
conjure up at very short notice. She gave the
merest of nods.

'Ooooh!' said half of them.

'Wow!' said the other half, as if the
penny was dropping.

'Hooray for Hell!' cried the Little
Ones.

And *Oh, gods,* thought Lief, *she's going to be insufferable now.*

Sometime later, Lief stretched his legs out towards the burning embers of the fire and wondered if he'd ever been so full before in his life.

'If I eat any more,' said Kran, 'I'm gonna puke … then I'll probably start eating all over again. That stuff was bloody **scrumptious**!'

Nolly burped like a bullock and the Little Ones giggled sleepily. Hell looked up from the sword, which she'd been hunched over for the last hour, rubbing at it with a mixture of grass and grit. It still looked just as rusty as when they'd found it on the beach.

'Go to sleep,' she said and, for a moment, Nolly looked confused, as if she'd been talking to him.

'Awwww,' the Little Ones knew exactly who she'd been referring to. They clambered up from around the fire and wobbled over to the shelter where Nuria and Etta had made sleeping pallets from thick wads of rushes and grass.

Lief felt like stretching his legs, so he got up too and walked slowly to the edge of the ruined courtyard. He rested his head on a broken parapet and stared into the night. To the south, the waves on the shore could be heard rolling in and sucking out. In spite of his recent memories, the sound was oddly comforting.

Lief stared roughly north where the Gauts had their watery camp and moored that ship of theirs in the estuary. Lief could see nothing in that direction save for a thin flash of silver where the halfmoon reflected on the water. But he felt the danger. To the west he could make out the dark pink fringe of the dying day on the horizon. To the east where his home had been was nothing but sea. And here he was, in the middle, a temporary sanctuary with a temporary family. Or could it become more than that?

It had been hard work, but it was the first good day he could recall in ages. The children needed a leader, safety, warmth, and comfort. They needed a home because theirs had all been lost – and this new place could be it. Hell obviously thought so. Frankly, he'd never seen her be so happy … or be so nice to him. He had a pretty good idea why. She had a chance to build what she never had in the village: a family. And Lief felt that now-familiar clench on his heart: his family! He would not give up on his old home.

Yet, even as he thought about that, he could see he was needed here in a way that he had never been in the village, where most of the time he was ignored and a bit useless. In Vantage it was the opposite. There was still so much to do: water to be collected, lookouts to be posted, walls repaired – if they could salvage enough stone.

And there was something else: Lief had riddles to solve. The crown didn't feel so peculiar anymore, he was getting used to it, but Lief knew that sooner or later he'd have to work out why he could hear the voice and – more to the point – what was this thing it spoke of that was waking? But that could wait until tomorrow.

As he trudged up the hill, towards his own bed, he heard Hell singing to the Little Ones.

[HELL]
*My comfy cot was made for me*
*To sail upon a sleepy sea.*
*Softly pillows on this bed,*
*Where I'll rest my weary head.*
*And I'll float off to distant lands,*
*Of sunny hills and sleepy sands.*

## Chapter 6: Storm Horizons

[BARD]
*Now my song it comes of age,*
*The words call out from every page,*
*'Neath silver hues and cobalt sky,*
*'Vantage rises, rejoice!' they cry.*

*But rejoice not I*

*For under skies of such good cheer,*
*Forces rise of dread and fear,*
*And this would happen by and by.*
*And this is how beginnings die.*

*So rejoice not I*

Lief woke and studied Etta in the morning sunlight. The thick mop of blond hair that usually fell across his forehead had swept back in his sleep to reveal an ugly scar, still pinkish and sore-seeming. Lief wondered how he got it. It was a clean cut – it could have been a blade. On the other hand, Lief was sure Etta wouldn't say if he asked what had happened. He knew very little about

this new tribe they were forming – how they
had all found themselves here, foreigners all,
and who they really were. All they'd had was
a good first day.

Lief got up and went outside to stir
some life into the fire. He added some dry
twigs and blew on the embers that still
smouldered in the ashes. Before long the fire
was popping and crackling cheerfully, taking
the edge off the morning damp.

He would discover as much as he
could about them all today.

'So we were out fishing with my granddad,
'cos my dad was at home with The Scourge,
what you call the plague round us – people
had been coming out in terrible sores – huge
boils that made you rave … then it killed
you. But the rest of us still needed to feed
ourselves. So, there we were and there was a
bit of a squall that pushed us out to sea – not
far – but further than usual … here, give us
a hand with this Your Royally Highness.'
Lief, Kran and Fran had formed a three-
person work party to clear the patches of
bramble and briar closest to the shelter.
Nolly had teamed up with Etta again and
they were busy extending the shelter to form

sleeping cells and cutting a hole in the roof for a fire in winter. Nuria and Hell were with the Little Ones, looking for water – preferably a proper spring or, better still, a well of some sort. Asking Kran about her life before they came here had been easy – you just pointed her at a conversation and she was off.

'… anyway, when the wee storm cleared, there was thick cloud about and Grandad's eyesight was never the best, so we was lost, just bobbing about … and then we saw this ship: low and fast in the water. We hoisted a sail because it looked like trouble and even tried to row but that thing's as swift as the wind, and silent. Before we knew it, they were on us. There was nothing we could do, even if we had warriors. The Gauts are huge, and their faces! Gobs like monsters! I've heard the folk say all the fight just goes out of you to look at them, you're so filled up with fear, and I know what they mean. Grandad was brave – he tried to protect us with his billhook – but they just reached over and grabbed Fran and me.'

'And your grandfather?' Lief asked. But he already knew the answer: the temperature in the glade plummeted.

'They chopped him in half and threw his body over the side. And Fran hasn't had a word to say for herself since.'

She took a deep breath and paused before going on. 'Anyway, until you came along, we didn't really know what to do. We were all going to go home – though how, I don't know, and if the Gauts have been there, I'm not sure there's anything to go back to. And …' Kran looked around, her eyes damp, 'this isn't a bad place to call home, is it now?'

Lief had no idea how he was going to respond to Kran. Before he had to think of something, he was saved by Hell.

'Look!' She cried out in a tone as if to say, *behold!* Her voice came from underneath an archway that had been entirely covered in thick, reddish ivy until Hell had taken her sword to it earlier. It now hung in festoons across the mouth of a dank tunnel.

[BARD]
*Oh! in spaces dark, this fortress fast,*
*Would by and by reveal its past.*

Lief got to the entrance just before Etta, and stopped dead in his tracks as the crown throbbed with a half vision: hollow sounds came from the dark corners of the passageway, as if long-buried in the stone.

He heard cries of fear, smelled smoke and, at the back of his throat, tasted the acidic taste of the dread all people feel when they know they are going to die. Then, as quickly as it came, the vision and the sense of panic it brought subsided.

Lief's flashback had made him pause but Etta had stopped, too. The darkness, the smell of damp stone and oppressive air of great age – and *something* else – was overbearing. Then pride got the better of both boys and they took the worn staircase that led down into the passage together.

The stairs were steep.

The first thing Lief thought was: *great!* as he rounded a corner that opened into a circular chamber: Hell had found the stronghold's main well. Light from a hole they had not noticed above ground shone down onto the ornately-carved stonework around the well. His second thought was: *gods, what's that?*

Each carving was separated into a panel and each panel depicted scenes of war. Men on horses charged bands of creatures who were rampaging wildly: smashing, burning and killing. The men wore armour and had stern looks but they seemed no match for the huge, heavily-muscled beasts, who walked on two legs but looked more like wild animals with huge manes of hair, fish mouths and needle teeth. Gauts.

Glancing sideways at Etta, seeing the pain and pent anger stamped on his face, Lief knew, without having to ask, what the other boy's story was. By his clothes, his speech and his features, they were from the same place that had been washed away and their fates could easily have been the same. He cleared his cloggy throat.

'The Plague had already come for some of us. I think the Gauts were on their way to our settlement, too. If the wave hadn't come when it did we could have been next.'

'But you weren't!' spat Etta. For a moment, Lief thought the boy's fury was about to be directed at him. He braced himself for physical contact, but stood his ground.

'We've all lost people,' Lief said as evenly as possible, 'those closest to us have all gone. We have to make the best of it.' Slowly, Etta's fury subsided, but his intensity remained.

'Oh, I'll make sure you do.' He bought his face close to Lief's. He was a hand taller but one thing fighting with Hell half his life had taught him: show no weakness. Lief held Etta's gaze without returning any of its anger.

A passing frown that may have been doubt fell across Etta's features, then he simply turned on his heel and stalked away.

'I don't know why you bother with him.' Hell emerged from the shadows.

'Because, thanks to you, caring about people's feelings – even the ones who hate me – is my job now.' And, with that, he made to leave the dark chamber filled with even darker memories.

'There's more down here,' Hell's voice was low, but he knew that tone well. Lief stopped and turned.

'What?'

'Look at the walls and let your eyes get used to the shadows. Then you'll see.' Lief forced his gaze away from the shafts of sunlight and into the dark corners.

[BARD]
*Kingdoms must to wax and wane,*
*For nothing, no-one stays the same:*
*Fortunes fall, fortress to dust,*
*And ships will hulk and swords to rust*
*For everything must die.*

*The Seven were forged to keep at bay,*
*The dreadful tread of Death's decay:*
*For fortunes rise, fortress be fast,*
*Ships can soar and swords outlast*

*For not everything must die.*


'OK,' said Lief, eventually looking up from the dim carvings, 'scary large dragon … there's a man holding a sword, an older man with a crown drinking out of an old cup, a boat and a big chicken.'

'Even you've heard the Song of the Seven.'

'Yeesss,' said Lief doubtfully, knowing where this was going, but not liking it.

'Let me remind you: a chariot that makes invincible all who ride it into war, the crown that gives great wisdom and insight to kings, the greatest sword ever forged, Jason's ship, the Cup of Life, the phoenix that can never die, and – in case you really are missing the obvious – the cauldron that fills with food.'

'You're not seriously saying the Seven are here?'

'Yes, I am, and I think they're the reason the wave sent us. You saw what happened last night, what the cauldron did.' Then she smiled at him – something that Lief was still struggling to get used to.

'Yes …' Lief had to admit he hadn't got close to understanding what had happened the night before. It all seemed like a feverish dream. Then again, everything had felt unnatural since they had been swept away. That is to say, everything felt *momentous*, as if they were at the very centre of things. But that was absurd.

Lief let his mind wander.

It was like they were in their own song – normally sung of gods and heroes – as if being here in Albion, finding Vantage, rebuilding the stronghold, the Gauts … But that was just ridiculous! No bards ever made songs about people like him.

Lief stared at the final panel. It showed a great beast rising up, attacking the Gauts who fell back in terror. 'And is that a *dragon*? I didn't think they existed.' He shivered, remembering the first words the crown spoke to him … the dragon's breath? The words had sounded ominous and heavy with meaning without him fully understanding why.

'This land was once great,' said Hell ignoring him. 'It will rise again but not without the treasures… as I have always said, you have an important destiny, Lief the Lesser.'

Hell didn't help.

After the chamber and its troubling carvings, Lief had spent the rest of the day with the others clearing what must have been the stronghold's main courtyard. It felt good to concentrate on mundane things – things that you could make better with simple, physical work. By midday, they had torn out the weeds and creepers that grew from the walls. After a short rest and some food, they set to work scraping away the matted moss and years of mulchy leaves that clogged the stone flags covering the surface of the courtyard end to end.

The sun lost heat, became bleary around the edges and deflated below the horizon. They still had a ruin on their hands, but it was their ruin. And it was one where they could see the walls (and that they needed repairing), the floor and – enticingly – the entrances to two more tunnels leading gods knew where.

Finally, they set about burying the old King within the walls. Feeling it only right, Lief took on most of the work and, by the end, the hole he managed to scrape out was respectable: deep enough to stand in waist-hcight. Once they had placed the King's mummified remains in the hole and covered it with spent earth, Nolly placed a large stone over the mound and the Little Ones put flowers around the edges.

They all stood around for a bit wondering what should happen next until it occurred to Lief he should say something. He'd just opened his mouth but Hell beat him to it.

> [HELL]
> *I see you, DEATH!*

She shouted, glaring at the dark places under the trees, making everyone jump,

> *Veiled Wraith! High-stepping ... near!*

then look about with alarm, peering into the same shadows as Hell – who was just warming up.

> *Yelping songs in your frozen breath.*
> *Your dark mists crowd the air.*
>
> *I roam through The Silent Place,*
> *You follow from dark pool to bent tree.*
> *Come! fold me in your shroud embrace,*
> *Let your breath suck mine from me.*

Not surprisingly everyone made a quick exit after that, leaving Lief and Hell alone. Lief pretended to survey the new structure Nolly had built, then the fire and its cooking area, the courtyard, the walls and the leagues of patch-worked countryside rolling out beyond … but he felt hyper-aware of Hell lately. She was different.

'That was … um, interesting,' was all he could think of saying. Hell's pale skin reddened.

'It's what they expect, now.' She smiled thinly. 'Didn't mean it to come out quite so melodramatic.' And *'gods'* thought Lief, *'that's it – she's nice to me, these days!* Nicer, anyway. They stood for what seemed like a bit too long in weird silence.

'It's looking good, isn't it?' he said, pointing at the shelter. For something to say.

'Not too bad,' she conceded after a pause. She was standing quite close to Lief.

But he didn't move away.

'Thanks,' he murmured. Then they both watched Etta, as if he was the most fascinating thing in the world, as he climbed the highest part of the wall and made a start on what was to be the first guard duty, keeping a careful eye on the Gauts' camp. They would all take it in turns to act as lookouts during the day and at night. That was the plan. The Little Ones had also said they wanted to keep lookout and Lief had agreed, as long as there was always one of the older kids on duty, too. That way, everyone felt involved. Now Hell was leaning down, rubbing a bare leg that was scratched by thorns. Lief tried not to look at her knees. He'd never really noticed Hell's knees before ... he quickly looked at the top of her head, instead. How the fine hairs on the nape of her neck parted to show the soft skin below ... this was worse.

But he didn't move away.

'The fort must have seemed like it was made by the gods when it was new,' Hell said, looking up. Lief did not reply; he knew what Vantage looked like when it was pristine thanks to the crown and his hallucinations, but he wasn't about to tell Hell about those. Not yet. Mentally, he superimposed the scene from his first flashback onto the one laid before them. Where Etta was standing, looking out towards the marshes, there had been a wooden platform. He would ask Nolly about making one tomorrow, one that looked over the trees. Hell bent down again. Her dark hair smelled of mint and curled up at the ends. He'd never noticed that before, either. When she straightened up, their faces were almost touching. She gave him a quizzical look.

But he didn't move away.

'Can we go now?' The Littlest Little One was looking up at Hell. There were still a couple of hours of daylight left, and Hell had promised an excursion down to the beach.

'Of course! Down to the beach before supper, we shall guess the language of the gulls and read the future in the tides.'

As she moved away, Lief followed. Because.

### [HELL]

*I'd like a field.*
*A large, green one.*
*And I'd walk across it alone,*
*On sunny days,*
*For the feel of wet legs,*
*From the bright drops of dew,*
*As the white sheep gently graze.*

*I'd like a trough,*
*Of cold, clean water.*
*And I'd plunge my head,*
*Deep, deep under.*
*Then I'd open my eyes*
*and watch the bubbles go up.*
*Sparkling silvery as they rise.*

*I'd like a big beach,*
*Full of bright, round pebbles from end to*
*end.*
*And frothy,*
*From the crashing waves.*

*And I'd sit and watch them.*
*And eat toffee.*

*And I'd like to see for thousands of miles.*
*To look at the world*
*down a great hill, a steep hill.*
*Spying on the valleys and hedges,*
*Rich with grass and pine;*
*Each detail a new discovery, to be*
*remembered.*

*And mine.*

They sat on the shoreline, looking out at the sea as it sloshed back and forth. Hell recited the words of a song Lief had not heard before, but it seemed familiar. That was it, Lief realised – the song summed up what was new about this place and old: a bit like home but beautiful, different but with just enough of what was recognisable to make it easy to like. Like Hell: she was basically the same. But altered. The way she was with the Little Ones, her fun and her new softness. The way she was with Lief, even that had changed, or perhaps he was just noticing what was always there. She had sought him out back at their home. Lief had always thought it was to make his life a misery but perhaps there was something else in it … he remembered waking to find her close to him on the log.

As they walked back up to Vantage tired, hungry, but content, Hell dropped back and Lief slowed his pace to match. There was a kind of pressure in the air between them and he felt fuzzy between his ears. Ever so slowly he edged towards Hell as his steps fell in with hers. Ever so slowly she seemed to move towards him, too.

'Hell,' he whispered.

'Lief?'

Here goes, he thought and he reached out his hand and took hers. It felt soft and dry. It felt like discreet intensity. Lief moved closer so her shoulder brushed his. Then … then … suddenly it hit him that he had absolutely no idea what the *then* was. What did he do next? He felt his hands start to sweat. He breathed in sharply and Hell's fingers spasmed. Like a flinch.

Oh, gods.

The silence that had been comfortable moments before quickly became anything but. Lief knew he should say something or the situation was only going to get worse, so he blurted out the first thing that came to mind.

'Er, I've been getting visions. I think it's the crown, or it's reacting to me.' He waited for a response but Hell was silent. It didn't matter, though, because now Lief had started talking it was surprisingly hard to stop. 'Yes, I don't think it's just the crown – perhaps I'm a See'er, like you?' He thought that sounded interesting … and grown up, but he felt Hell's silence get, if anything, worse. 'Maybe we both have a gift,' he said brightly. Now it felt like he was gabbling. 'And maybe it's only starting to come out now … now that we're getting, you know, older.' Lief risked a glance at Hell and was alarmed. She had a frown line across her forehead. Lief tried to change the subject – perhaps she found the idea of visions disturbing. He thought of something reassuring to say. 'We've done so much together. I think that when I take the Gauts' ship and sail home we should offer to take everyone … now that I am King.'

Her hand whipped away.

'Oh?' Hell spun round. The look on her face hit Lief like an open-handed slap. 'Go on.' Lief knew that tone from the age of five. It meant *tread very carefully*.

'I, er, as leader,' actually Lief had no idea what he was going to say in the first place, let alone now that it seemed essential to say something important. 'I decide where we go …' he stopped and swallowed, '… *we* should perhaps start … um, planning how to capture the ship …' Hell looked properly furious. '… as king …' he finished pointlessly.

Something seemed to break between them.

'King?' There was a thunderclap … well, probably not, but it felt like it. Hell was pale, '… King! *Fool*, more like! For your information, I'm not going anywhere: we rid this land of Gauts, for this is our land now, and we stay to rebuild. What do you think we've been doing for the last three days?' But Lief couldn't believe what she was saying. He didn't want to argue, now that they had seemed to have become friends, but this was the old Hell back. Worse.

'We can't defeat the Gauts. You never actually believed that, did you?'

'With all my soul, and I believed you did, too. What about your speech on the first day? *We are few, but we start to fight back from this day, this day of days.* They believed you, *really* believed you, even I believed you … you know, I actually thought you might be turning into the person you always were meant to be.' She went to move off and instinctively, Lief tried to take her hand again. She let him but it felt like something dead now. Hell watched his face fall as her expression went from furious to mocking. 'So you thought you'd hold my hand and I'd do exactly as you say … and then what?

95

Perhaps I'd kiss you?' She made a horrible pouty face, 'like this? Then we'd hold hands some more and then something else … and then what? I'd be your wife soon enough and be grateful, because you're a *king* and of course you'd tell me what to do, and we'd sail back to that wasteland of nothing but grass in every direction that you think is so special, where people will leave you to starve if your parents die … and I'd get fat with children in that place and red in the face and hands from washing? That's your plan is it?'

'No, I …' *Where in the gods had this come from?* If Lief ever wished with all his heart he could start again it was now. A small part of him wanted something terrible to happen, like another wave – to erase the last minute and a half from their memories, ' I like you … we…,' he started to say.

'*We*? There is no we, Lief – and you're not a real king, just remember that. I don't know what gave you that impression. And I don't know what gave you the impression I care about *you*. At *all*. For your information, Your Royal Big-headedness, the only thing I care about right now are the Seven Treasures, using them to defeat the Gauts and to undo what has happened. That is it. I won't run away and I won't be someone's wife. I do not belong to you Lief the Lesser, just because of that stupid crown on your head and …,' she paused, '… your stupid visions that probably aren't real,' she hissed. She started to stalk off as Lief made to go after her. Hell stopped and turned.

'I've said it before, go your own way, Little Lief. I'll go mine.'

She marched up the hill, leaving Lief feeling more on his own in the gathering gloom than he had ever felt.

He stood there for ages: what had just happened? She seemed so changed this evening and for a second he was sure her hand had squeezed his back. So what had he misunderstood? One minute they felt so close, then he'd mentioned the king thing … it was probably a stupid thing to say, but Hell said pretty weird or dumb things all the time and he was willing to overlook that! And he'd never said he'd stay, he'd always made it clear he would leave to find his parents. Except… he knew that wasn't quite the case. These last few days he'd even caught himself daydreaming about making Vantage into a proper castle, as it had been before in all its shimmering, majestic glory, defeating the Gauts and becoming a real King … with a Queen: Hell.

Lief felt like curling up into a ball. What had he been thinking? Him and Hell?

He made to walk up the hill, then remembered what she'd said, and thought about going back down to the beach – but why would he do that? In the end, he just sat on a fallen log and stared at the waves between the sea. By and by, perplexity gave way to brooding and brooding to anger.

[LIEF]
*We travelled far together,*
*From a life we had to flee*
*But when I show I like you*
*It's fine you can't stand me!*

*We're all that's left of us*
*- Rescued by a tree!*
*So, of course, if I should care for you*
*Why should you care for me?*

*From now I'll keep my trap shut,*
*From now I'll leave you be,*
*I'll take the feelings I have left,*
*And drown them in the sea.*

He wasn't much of a bard, but he was angry, and he felt better for saying it.

It was properly cold now, and Lief was stiff when he got up and began to walk back to Vantage. He would just ignore Hell now, which would not be hard – he'd been doing his best to ignore her for years. That was an easy decision to make. Much harder was the question about whether he would stay now. After this. Or go? Was there anything to go back for, or was Hell right, was it all gone, swept away and his family drowned? At least with Vantage he had something to build on. Lief refused to admit it, but it was beginning to feel like a home and the others felt like a family. Here he was someone, too. At home he was just Lief the Lesser, who everyone ignored.

And if he somehow was able to leave, Hell would almost certainly still lead a frontal attack on the Gauts and get them all killed.

Lief took a deep breath. He would stay for now: if only to play the cautious king and make sure they didn't do anything stupid and die in doing so. Who could tell – perhaps the crown would provide him with an answer. Perhaps the Gauts would go away on their own and this new sea disappear. Then things could go back to being the way they were … except without Hell.

Lief had to admit, this seemed unlikely. It felt more like nothing would ever be the same again.

As he went through the narrow gap and into the courtyard he saw Hell, Nolly, Etta, Nuria – everyone – standing on the wall, looking out at something towards the marshes, their faces lit in strange red light: taut with worry and, worse, with fear.

And, instantly, he knew that something was very wrong.

[BARD]
*Through seas of granite - grey and harsh,*
*To Albion's foothold, this blasted marsh.*
*The brasiers burn, the Gauts will feast*
*- blackened mutton for Trollhaten Beast!*

*From lands of ice and molten spew,*
*Upon shore ships retch their rotten crew.*
*The brasiers burn, as Gauts will feast*
*- fair Albion for Trollhaten Beast!*

## Chapter 7: Walls

The night was clear and the light came early. Before it reached the tops of the trees surrounding the courtyard, the morning sun had burned off any vestiges of cloud in the east.

The previous evening, the children had watched in silent dismay as three ships had breached the marshes, each teeming with more monstrous shadows: grey-green Gauts, strutting on two legs like men, but huge and brute – like beasts who had learned to walk, the better to invade and conquer. They jumped ashore and roared challenges at the perishing sun, at the new land and at the puny humans who cowered at their arrival.

Lief had barely slept and was on the wall long before the dawn, watching three ships slip anchor and head north, all with skeleton crews, leaving their cargo of ground troops behind.

Very shortly after, the bulk of this new army broke camp. Marching west.

'I've seen this before, the ships are returning to fetch more monsters from the

Ice Lands.' Nuria wrapped both her arms about her body as if to protect herself.

Part of Lief had hoped that they would all leave and be someone else's problem. The force that stayed in the marsh camp were the Gauts from the original ship that he had seen with Hell on the first day, acting as a welcoming party for new invaders.

Take them out, and it would be a blow to an enemy that had no fear. But how? It seemed impossible. Escape was still their best option in Lief's view.

'Look how they murder the Land.' Nuria spat. 'What they do not kill, they poison.'

And it was true: now it was light, Lief could see the area where they spent the night was blackened. The marsh grasses had withered and a sickly grey scum floated on the surface of the water.

'It was the same when they came to the far south, to my homeland. They landed and came ashore. Our warriors met them on the beach but they cut them down so easy, like they were harvesting wheat. The sand was covered in blood. Then they came inland and took slaves and our shelter. But they have to keep moving. When they stole me, I was moved four times. With each moon cycle, everything around them becomes grey, then black and dies. Nothing will grow, even the animals to hunt die – or flee. Like here. There is no food, so they have to move on. It is like their home: nothing lives, it is only cold and bitterness. It is Niflheim, the Land of the Dead.'

'How did you escape?'

'We were lucky. When the wave came, the one that brought you here, their ship tore its moorings and was swept away. In the chaos, we were swept away too, and ended up at the foot of this hill. Quite a few of us were drowned.' Nuria's eyes squinted in the face of the rising sun. 'I'm the last of the children from my country.'

'I'm sorry,' was the best he could say.

Nuria glanced at him and blinked and tried to smile.

'But we survived and we're here … and you came with Hell, who is …' Nuria paused and thought, ' … she is everything I wish to be sometime. And we have hope.'

Lief half smiled back but it was hard even hearing Hell's name. The crown gave a sharp jab and light flashed through his temples where the rim rested. It felt like it was burning a hole through the sockets of his eyes.

[BARD]

*Dread darkness comes by three:*
*The first is sickness, the second sea.*
*The third from lands of ice and thunder,*
*With bloody axe to cleave asunder.*

When Lief's senses returned, he was surprised he was still standing. Would he ever get used to these visions and voices that came without warning? His arms had locked and he was gripping the parapet harder than he thought possible. Nuria touched his shoulder. 'Lief, um, *Sire*? What is it?'

But Lief ignored her. Instead he stared across the pools of marsh to where he could see the largest Gaut of all standing motionless, facing in their direction. It was looking with vicious intensity towards Lief. Slowly, and very deliberately, it raised a clawed fist.

Up until now, Lief's nightmares had had no voice.

Yet the howl that reached them across the marsh was the insanity that festered in the darkest pit of his soul.

Hell was in full fighting mode.

'We go there tonight and burn that ship of theirs. We show them they can't come and go as they please. Make them fear. Hurt *them*.'

'I don't think that's a good idea,' said Nolly slowly, as if deep in thought. Lief kept silent for now.

'I swear to the gods that ship's possessed,' Kran looked at Fran who nodded. 'When we was on it, it seemed to sail itself. All the Gauts did was sit around and drink and kill things. It's not Gautish; their boats are heavy in the water, for fighting. This one is built for speed and it's enchanted. The sails and the ropes and everything on it sing to each other. It's like it flies through the water – and they stole it from somewhere, that's for sure.'

'But we have to do something,' said Etta, 'we can't just hide up here for the rest of our lives. Or run anymore.'

'Precisely, who'd want to do that?' Hell said acidly and Lief tried not to catch her eye.

'Surely they will move eventually?' Nuria was obviously uncomfortable disagreeing with Hell but she was scared – and rightly so.

Lief cleared his throat, everyone (except Fran) had had their say, and it was up to him to make a judgment.

'My father was a warrior.' Out of the corner of his eye he saw Hell scowl, but she had the decency to keep quiet. 'He said only a fool takes a stronger enemy before he knows his weakness. He also said good defences were as important as a good attack. Right now we know they want land and they need slaves, and they know we are here. We also know that everything they touch seems to die, that must mean something. We need to find out more … *but* …,' he saw Hell start to open her mouth, '… but most importantly we need to strengthen Vantage. I say the Gauts will eventually lose their fear of this place, or their need for slaves will become greater and they will come up the hill looking for us. Vantage needs to be as strong as it has ever been.'

'But there will be only one way to defeat the Gauts, once and for all,' Hell stated.

'What's that?' several people said at once in slightly different ways: hopeful.

'Magic.' Several of the same people looked disappointed. Hell looked exasperated. 'The Gauts think they are invincible, but nothing conquers magic. You've all seen what the cauldron can do.' Everyone looked at their feet, it was one thing having a magic cauldron, but no-one could see how that was going to help kill ogres.

'Thank you,' said Lief and a small part of him felt good that the others seemed to agree with him. And not Hell. He cleared his throat. 'So whilst we're waiting for fairies and hobgoblins to rescue us,' there were a few smiles and even titters from the Little Ones and Hell looked murderous, which felt even better. ' … we need to fix the walls, block the tunnels and mount extra guards – especially at night. No more trips to the beach: we work, eat and rest, then work again.' He put on his stern face. 'Even you Little Ones need to help.' They all nodded very seriously. 'Those on guard duty, watch the Gauts, count their numbers, see where they go, what they do, what they eat. Anything that could help us fight them. Because the day will come – and soon – when we will need to. But remember, if our defences are strong, they cannot hurt us.'

> [LIEF]
> *Can magic build a wall, mend a wheel,*
> *What does it do, is it real?*
> *Does it come from hell or heavens above,*
> *Does magic care, does magic love?*
>
> *It fools our hearts, our minds, our eyes!*
> *It might be clever, but is it wise?*
> *Can magic build a wall, mend a wheel,*
> *Can it fight a foe who's real?*

107

He looked at them all in turn as they nodded, and finished by smiling confidently at the Little Ones.

He even smiled at Hell.

[BARD]
*Hope, too, returns by three:*
*The first is I, the second we,*
*The third still slumbers, still hunkers deep*
*Yet now it stirs from cavernous sleep.*

And work they did. But with none of the former joy or enthusiasm of discovery, as during those first days: they were not so much bringing Vantage back to life as saving their own.

And no-one worked harder than Lief.

He rose long before dawn to ask about the Gauts with whoever had taken the night watch, then he would walk the walls whilst it was still dark, checking for signs that the Gauts were on the move. Hell had set traps and snares that would trigger if Gauts attempted to launch a surprise attack under cover of the trees.

The others would get up at first light. After a short breakfast, mostly eaten in silence, they would split into two groups: one carrying stone to holes and rents in the walls, the other matching the stones to the gaps and filling them as best they could. Nolly and Etta acted as foremen for the different gangs.

After lunch, they swapped tasks. Then, as it got dark, Hell and Nuria would venture beyond the walls to set more traps and check the ones already laid. Etta would supervise the cutting and planting of sharpened stakes into the ground. Whilst they were out in the open, the lookouts were tripled, in case the Gauts attempted a grab strike.

In between times, Hell practised obsessively with her sword. As for the others, Nuria had made a sling, which she used to launch small rocks with surprising accuracy. Fran and Kran tried to make bows, but with less success. Even Etta and Nolly took time to make themselves a collection of dangerous-looking spears and clubs.

Only Lief remained weaponless.

All through the long hours of work, the bellows and howls of the Gauts never let up. They were clearly on edge: it was as if they were steeling themselves, but it was also as if they were in pain.

Lief had taken to wearing the crown all the time now, even at night. Part of him couldn't stand to wear it, another part could not imagine being without it. The crown gave him terrible dreams of Gauts: so vivid it felt as if he was inside their heads, treading through marsh, hiding from light and howling in anger – and something else?

It wasn't just that they wanted revenge, or they wanted their slaves back. From what the crown had shown him in his visions, Lief was sure the fear they felt of this place came from some ancient memory: of battles with the warriors who once ruled here, and it rankled them and they would seek to overcome this fear, and overcome the children, before moving inland to join with the rest of their forces.

Kran had been right on the first day, something was wrong with them. And Lief wondered what that was, because it could be the clue to defeating them.

He also dreamt of scales and claw, smoke and heat. Of a huge beast that had not yet stirred … and might never.

[BARD]
*But conjuring or mighty sword,*
*Is powerless within discord,*
*For then that which hunkers deep,*
*Will never stir from potent sleep.*


Up until now, the Little Ones had been the only source of genuine laughter in the stronghold, but the Gauts' howling and raging began to make them fearful and quiet.

Hell did her best to cheer them up in the evenings with songs and stories and it helped for a while. Lief would watch and listen and try not to think back to that evening, the unresolved argument, what she had said to him and – most of all – he tried not to think about how holding her hand held felt.

Every so often he would catch her glance at him with an odd look on her face he could not read. She would see him notice her looking and look away.

The only time they spoke was to argue.

'This work is a waste of time.'

'Not when it saves lives.'

'It'll just prolong the moment we are taken and killed,' Hell shot back, and Lief wanted to yell at her, but the atmosphere in the stronghold was bad enough without a full-blown argument.

'So what should we be doing?'

'You know. We should be listening to ancient wisdom, uniting the treasures and harnessing their power. It is the only way.'

'How can you be so sure of something that you've never seen and can't prove even exists – apart from a few pictures on a well and your over-active imagination?'

'Because I believe and in belief, there is power.'

'That doesn't even mean anything, Hell – it just sounds a bit … mysterious and impressive. You keep up with the traps and I'll finish the walls.'

And almost finished they were. Vantage's walls were now as high as they ever had been, its entrances sealed, the foot of the stronghold bristling with spikes like it was some prehistoric creature risen from the sea, and the woods were lethal.

They were as ready as they would ever be, but though the Gauts clamoured, still they did not come.

Lief took to prowling the parapets all the time now. He wanted them to attack, for something to happen, because life cooped up in the castle – the sullen atmosphere, ignoring Hell – was becoming unbearable. At the same time, he dreaded them coming. They weren't fighters, they were children, with only one sword between them, wielded by someone who thought something you couldn't see – or even rely on – would solve everything.

## Chapter 8: Angreb

[BARD]
*The Human Heart's a vacant house,*
*Dark chambers and closed doors –*
*With shutters on its windows,*
*Broken stairs between the floors.*

*Inside every Human Heart,*
*Sequestered from the sun,*
*Someone sits alone inside –*
*Very often, very young.*

*It's the child that lives within us,*
*Who huddles and hopes and waits.*
*But age and rage have built this house,*
*Put chains upon the gates.*

*It is the child in all of us,*
*Who trusts for others to be kind –*
*No house is built a fortress,*
*I think you'll often find.*

*For once the doors are open,*
*Once light fills it end to end,*
*This loving heart will never close,*
*Whatever you pretend.*

Days passed.

It was cold and the world around Vantage was swamped in darkness as Lief was standing looking out towards the Gauts' camp one morning. The air smelled of rain and smoke, which signalled summer was drawing to an end. He contemplated the coming autumn and what a winter under siege might mean.

A figure to his left moved out of the shadows. Hell.

Lief wondered how long she had been there, watching him, before he reminded himself that he wasn't caring these days.

'We need to talk, Lief,' she said.

'Honestly, Hell, if it's about the treasures again, or spells or destiny – yours or mine …'

'It's about us.' Lief felt his mouth twist into a bitter smile in the dark.

'You said there is no us.'

'Yes, no … I mean,' Lief could feel Hell's frustration mirror his own. Good, he thought. Hell sighed, '… We have to agree … even if there was something to go back for, I don't know why you'd want to, people there never saw anything in you.'

'What, so just because you were the only one who did means I should do what you want? It doesn't work like that.'

'I know.' Hell was annoyed, now. 'But going back won't prove anything to them – you'll always be Lief *the Lesser* in their eyes.'

'And yours, too – in spite of what you keep saying.'

'That's not fair!'

'Fair is giving people a choice and you never gave me one. You just saddled us with a bunch of orphans because you like playing the hero and it was me that had to try and work out a way of looking after them, when I wanted to go home. I never heard you mourn our home, the people, your own brother!'

'Gods, Lief! Everyone I cared about died, then the village deserted me. And my brother …' Hell's voice almost cracked, 'he hurt me, in ways you don't know … and you don't want to know. But none of that matters now, here we've got something and I think I've changed … we've both changed. We've grown up because we had to – we had people counting on us.'

They stared at each other. And, for the first time, Lief allowed himself to understand why Hell believed in magic, not men, why she was so good with the Little Ones, why she wanted to stay and, most of all, why she never wanted to go back. He opened his mouth to say something ....

'Ship!' Nolly's voice from the seaward wall of Vantage cut through their connection like a cleaver.

And although he had been expecting this moment for nearly a whole moon cycle, although he was almost sure it would happen soon, the next words still came as a shock.

'They're coming!'

[BARD]
*The Gauts were fixed on gruesome quest for land and lives.*

*Sailing up from sodden coast, to wretched rocks, then shore,*

*They had crept on Vantage in the bitter dawn,*

*And beneath bloody skies bellowed battle cries.*

*I'm a selfish fool!* thought Lief, shame, anger and fear freezing him to the spot. He'd been wrong about Hell and wrong about the Gauts: there was to be no frontal assault – their ship had stolen around the peninsular in the night. They were launching an attack on them from behind – the beach had always been the weak point, he had just chosen to ignore it. Lief cursed himself – his stupid fight with Hell, one that should have been sorted days ago, had cost them precious time to prepare.

He turned to go but Hell grabbed his arm fiercely. 'Wait!' she said, 'there's something you need to know, in case …'

But Lief broke away.

[BARD]
*Howls of savagery and rage, like pain*
*that had oft struck fear in heroes,*
*Still less children, alone*
*and untested in war*
*and ways of men and monster!*

*Then Gauts leapt from enchanted ship,*
*Bronze greaves and iron sinew*
*that splashed through cold waves the height*
*of hills,*
*As these giants galloped ashore*
*with battle cry and ragged roar.*

Lief knew they had been badly caught unawares. He had a brief flashback to when their village had been raided and his father cut down: shouts of alarm from lookouts who had not been attentive, a rush of horses and large men in furs, of fire and of bronze meeting bronze in the darkness … He shook the memory away.

'Nolly!'

'Yes, Sire!'

'You take Etta and scout the walls, in case they're coming from the woods too!' Nolly nodded and Etta followed without a word.

'Everyone else, to the Sea Gate!'

*From Vantage, fear-brightened eyes*
*watched beast first breach head, then break*
*the shore,*
*To fall upon the broken trees and briar,*
*That led upwards, ever higher, to their*
*panicked prize.*
*As the grim demons hacked with pitted axe*
*and sword,*
*Their steady tramp become a charge full of*
*terrible glory.*

Lief watched the Gauts jump from their ship and pound up the seaward path towards Vantage. They were fast and confident …

*But short-lived!*

*For Hell's infernal traps had found their*
*mark,*
*And with it, Gauts found their measure:*
*Thundering war chants became howls:*

119

*First frustration as limbs were tangled*
*and Trollhaten toppled,*
*But then rage and fear.*

*For creatures from iron-hard land and*
*frozen sheets,*
*Where the sore Earth bleeds its fiery blood,*
*Loath gentle field and fern, brook and*
*branch.*
*To them it seemed the very land was rising*
*up,*
*In Nature's Repulse.*

*With no foe to fight, but forest to dread,*
*The Gauts' attack wavered,*
*And the children above watched*
*with hope rising in trusting hearts.*

'It worked!' Nuria cried, she grinned at Hell,
'our traps worked!' Hell nodded, but she
gripped her sword all the more tightly. Lief
felt his heart beat a brief, hopeful tattoo in
his chest but held back from saying
anything: this was just the first wave. He
turned to Kran.

'Loose arrows,' he said.

*And now flame-headed twins from Thrace*
*sent swarms of arrows from hunting bow,*

*That flew like ireful wasps,*
*In the hideous faces of their foe.*

*And Nuria, from dusty south,*
*Flung rock and shard*
*from sling shot true and hard.*
*And the Gauts line broke and fell back to*
*beach.*
*As the children rose and cheered.*

*All except Lief, the Lesser.*

He wanted to shout – he was on the brink of sharing the triumph of the others as the Gauts broke and ran but something told him to turn. It was the same sense that spoke of hidden danger in the dark, that woke him as a small child with nameless fears; the prehistoric awareness that said *beware the monsters that lurk, the gorgons you cannot see but sense*.

*For the crown on his head,*
*That weighed far heavier than its gold,*
*Had burst to life.*
*In thunder flash, it filled his head*
*with nightmares of Beast sliding under sea,*
*and under rock, through tunnel dark and*
*dangerous.*

*Strong limbs pushed through cold salt*
*currents clear,*
*And into caverns dank and drear,*
*And upwards still, to spring, then …*

*Well!*

*Lief turned, as the vision in his mind's eye*
*burned white hot.*
*He meant to shout,*
*'The Gauts will out!*
*Hell, Hell – beware the Well!'*

*But too late – for Lief had not yet mastery*
*of what he wore,*
*And the warning had come after, not before.*

*So Gauts burst from the tunnels,*
*Slopping water, chopping: keen on slaughter,*
*They charged the children.*

'Nolly, Etta!' he started to cry, for they were
closest to the cellar that contained the well,
but the words would not come out. Lief
staggered with the weight of the crown. *Not
now,* he wanted to scream at the damned circlet, *leave
me be … they need me.*

*And so Lief turned,*

*But still the wretched crown blistering*
*burned.*
*And his legs gave way.*

*Falling faint,*
*When most he was needed.*
*The Gauts had broken in, unheeded.*

*As he sank, oblivion covering him like a*
*shroud,*
*All he saw was Hell:*
*Marching forward, sword in hand, hacking*
*and glorious.*
*But Gauts reaching out with barks*
*victorious,*

*Gnarled hands grasping.*
*At the smallest.*

Hell fought to break through the line of
Gauts dripping with well water, to get to the
Little Ones. To protect them. She injured
the first warrior in her path and hacked the
sword out of another's claw until two more
crowded her, and cuffed her to the slippery
earth. She looked around, Nolly was still
fighting, as was Etta, but the Gauts just
brushed their blows aside. Fran and Kran
had run out of arrows and were throwing

rocks with Nuria. But the Gauts ignored them, too: grabbing the terrified Little Ones in pairs, they turned to the Seaward Gate. Hell looked for Lief in a panic and saw him lying on the ground, not moving. It was only then that she realised they had lost. It had all been over in minutes. At that moment, every battle she had ever fought seemed lost.

'Stop,' for the first time in her life, Hell pleaded. 'Please don't hurt them.'

She slipped in the mud, tried to rise and fell back again as she watched, in dismay, as the Gauts carried off the prize they had known all along was theirs for the taking.

Part of Hell's soul broke away and fell into darkness.

'Take me,' she tried to shout but it came out as a pitiful whisper, ' … take me … because I'm broken already …'

## Chapter 9: Lief the Lesser

When Lief woke, he was soaked to the skin. His bones felt brittle and it was as if the blood in his veins had been flushed away by cold water. Nolly's bruised face peered at his. 'He's alive!' said Nolly, 'the King's alive!' and Lief would have snorted in derision if only he had the energy. Slowly, he sat up and looked around.

Etta, Nuria, Fran and Kran were in a huddle, staring at nothing. Mute. They looked unharmed, which seemed like a miracle. Had Hell's counter attack worked? Suddenly Lief didn't feel so bad. But … an appalling awareness began to dawn on him. His head whipped round, as he searched the rest of the courtyard: dread crowding his thoughts.

'Where are the Little Ones?' he asked. But he already knew.

Eventually someone cleared their throat.

Kran's voice was hoarse, '… they ignored us, they just took the wee ones,' her face crumpled again, but she had no tears left.

Lief looked at his hands – they were covered in blood. Great splashes covered his shirt as well. Lief touched his face: his nose had been bleeding, that was all. He thought of nosebleeds as a childish thing and felt ashamed.

His head ached. Amazingly, the crown was still on it. He went to pull it off, but Nolly took him gently by the wrist.

'Don't, please,' he said, 'we need you.'

Lief opened his mouth to argue, then shrugged. He stood up; he had something to do.

Lief found Hell in the cellar with the carvings. He was relieved she wasn't hurt, or worse, but he couldn't think of a way of saying it. But he did need to talk to her.

She was crouched down by the well where the Gauts had broken through, as if to make herself as small as possible.

The crown had shown him how they would get in, how they did not need to breach Vantage's high walls but too late – or, more to the point, he had not been listening to it. Since the building work on the walls, Lief had been blocking the visions, when the crown could have saved them all along. They weren't hallucinations, they were prophecies, and he'd refused to recognise that just so he could prove a point about magic to Hell. Lief did wonder how many regrets he'd have accumulated by the time he became an old man: more than there were stars in the sky.

'The Gauts got in because we were no longer united,' he said, '… the magic is real, the crown showed me – I just didn't want to listen. I wanted you to be wrong so I could be right. The Gauts were always coming, not just for the Little Ones. Pretty soon they'll find out about the treasures. They need them to stay here … you were right about that, too.'

'Perhaps.' Hell did not look round. 'But they always knew how to get into Vantage. If I'd got behind your efforts to strengthen the defences, we might have thought of blocking the well.' Hell was bent, almost in a foetal position and Lief wondered if she was hurt, after all. 'I suppose they've been here before, or their ancestors.'

'They took the Little Ones because they give this place life and the Gauts need life to survive. I've finally worked it out, they don't want slaves, they want prey. Vantage feels empty.'

'Without the weak to protect it is no more than a shell – a folly.' Hell said matter-of-factly, she finally looked up at him. It was then he felt the anger coming off her, like heat. But that didn't even come close to the place where Lief was. 'You know what I hated about the skirmishes between villages when we grew up, the raids and now this fight for survival, this war?'

'No, I don't, Hell.'

'It's not that it's always the weakest who suffer the most, it's that they're the ones with no choice!' Hell was trembling. 'We should have protected them. That was our job!'

'I should have protected them.' Lief felt his own anger finally finding a vocal range, like a damp fire catching. But, unlike Hell, unlike any of them, the anger wasn't directed at the Gauts and what they did. It was directed at himself. All he had done when the Gauts broke through was faint. A small, spiteful voice at the back of his mind told him that he'd done so out of fear.

So he was here. Now he wanted what he came to this terrible place for, this dank pit of memory and regret. He wanted Hell to blame him, to rage at him – he was the so-called-King after all and it was his plan that they had followed, his leadership. Most of all, for the first time in his life, he wanted her to do what she had always done, to laugh at him for being small, ridiculous and … a coward.

But when he looked at her, for once there was no scorn.

Hell regarded him through unreadable eyes.

'Oh, Lief,' she said almost gently. 'If only *I* could be the person I am. Who I really am. I was angry that evening by the beach, but not with you – with myself. I'm not a great sorceress, or a Queen. I wield a sword, not a sceptre.'

What was she talking about? This wasn't why he sought Hell out. This wasn't what Hell was *for*. She should have mocked him, made him feel small, it was what he deserved. Fury built up inside him in waves, like one of the crown's assaults. Suddenly it was crystal clear, his rage had burned his thoughts to white-heat purity: Hell would never give him what he wanted. Or needed.

He grabbed the sword.

'What are you doing?'

What *was* he doing?

He teetered. He stared at the sword, then stared at Hell. 'I tell you what I am doing. I'm going my own way, like you said. I'm going down to get the Little Ones. I'm going to kill Gauts.'

'... then you'll die.'

'Good,'

'No,' Hell struggled upright. And that's when he saw the blood covering her arms and chest. But it just made it worse, made him want to kill Gauts even more: he couldn't stop himself, now.

'Tell me one reason why not!' His rage still made his thoughts pure but they were turning in a different direction. 'One reason why shouldn't I go. In your honest opinion, Hell, you tell me that.'

'I can't,'

'Won't.'

'No … it's …'

'What? Just spit it out. You're never normally shy when it comes to dishing out advice!'

'Oh, Lief, since we got here, since we lost everything … no, since before even all that, When my parents died and you stood up for me, I knew you were different. I watched you because you were the only person in our settlement who could lead without killing. And I was right. In these past few weeks you united us in ways I could not. I only see things because I've always been on the outside looking in and, if I see anything, it's that you have something important to do.' Hell took a deep, shuddering breath. 'But I used to get angry as well. You had everything: a mother, a father, family, and I had nothing. But you were going to do nothing but grow old in that place where nothing ever happened and no-one saw you for who you really were. If you go now with that sword, you're not coming back. And it might be heroic and what your idea of a king is but it's … it's too soon … people go … everyone goes … not you, of all people.'

Lief stared at Hell. He didn't know why she was saying all this. 'I'm wasting time,' he took the sword, 'I've got Gauts to butcher.'

'That's not you!'

'That's what kings are meant to do, isn't it? That's what you made me when you decided to tell everyone I was royalty!'

'You and I survived for a reason; don't throw your life away, it's not your path.'

[BARD]
*The moment it was needed,*
*The truest thing Hell ever said*

*went unheeded.*

'Here's the crown,' he spat out the words, 'you can be Queen, now. I can't be King, I'm pathetic.' He threw the crown on the ground and turned to go up the stairs and out the archway. He was striding across the grass courtyard when Hell caught his hand.

131

'You'll die, and we'll be alone. Lief
…' she paused, and all the pain and loss and
unused love was poured into her expression.
'I'll be alone!'

And that was just enough to make
him pause.

And that was just enough to make
Hell reach forward and pick the crown up
from the cold stone as Lief brought the blade
down on it with a shout of rage.

And, as crown and blade met, their
whole world exploded in light and ferocious
power.

[BARD]
*From time unwaking Lore has been*
*what binds us all, from King and Queen,*
*To tinker sleeping in a hedge,*
*or sparrow perching on a ledge.*

*For everyone and every creature,*
*Are nurtured by our Mother Nature.*
*From most low, to most sublime,*
*We're bound fast by Father Time.*

*But the dragon stirs and would be woken,*
*By deeds undone and words unspoken.*

When Lief woke for the second time that day, everything had changed. He was lying in the sunlight, on soft grass.

'Lief?' Hell looked different. Everything looked different. He stood, slowly. Hell, the sword in one hand, held his arm. And everyone knelt. Even Etta.

What had happened?

Lief concentrated. He had wanted to destroy the crown for that one moment: he remembered his rage all too clearly, but he also remembered the very moment rusty sword touched tarnished crown and they both seemed to … fuse. Until now, both sword and the crown had been mere objects. Lifeless and only useful in so far as the purpose they were made for: one for hacking, the other a bauble of vanity.

But now life and power beat from them in waves.

The sword in Hell's hand was no longer crusted bronze: its blade rippled like the evening sun on water. It seemed lighter in her hands, yet somehow more powerful. It said: *I am Infinite Menace*.

The crown's patina now had depth and age. It spoke to him of wisdom and kingship and the true meaning of what both meant. It finally showed him who he was or was meant to be.

Without needing to look, Lief saw every aspect of Vantage's safety swathed in Lore: how it was now and in brilliance before. He saw beyond the wall, beyond blasted marsh and sands, to the gentle hills and fertile lands, shielded from all that was harsh. He saw valleys that teemed with life and dappled woods crossed by sunbeams, chatty streams and birds in flight. He saw an ancient land and what lay asleep at its very core, from valley to cave to river and shore. He felt Albion's life fire: its protector who would be woken, by one who knew what words were spoken. He saw his past, *his place* and what the future could be. For one great moment he saw all there was to see.

But, mostly, he saw a way to defeat the Gauts.

## Chapter 10: Back

[BARD]
*That summer the grass had grown thick*
*and a little higher by the waters.*
*Fed by the floods,*
*The riverside lounged in a haze of green*
*Quietly content under a buttered sun.*

*And with the first flush of the season,*
*Curiosity beckoned Lief down to where*
*the flounced grass lay woven in this*
*Albion jungle of dandelion and cowslip.*

*And the air shifted slightly, to disclose*
*a path through the calm sense of repose.*
*And it seemed so absolute and guileless,*
*That amongst the heat he felt dizzy.*

*So he laid his head to rest between*
*an old oak's shoulder and gentle crook.*
*Disoriented and half asleep,*
*struck dumb by the exquisite sense of being*
*alive.*

*For now.*

This was very likely his last day on Earth,
but Lief felt perfectly calm – probably for
the first time in his life.

He had no idea whether he would stay in Albion or leave this place that felt more like home with every dew-drenched dawn and delicate sunrise.

However, he knew what he had to do and what kind of king he needed to be. Today, at least.

It was this sense of serenity that communicated itself to the others, so it seemed perfectly acceptable to rest in the heat of the late summer day, camped out in the grass, whilst they gathered their strength for the storm that was to come.

'We go whilst there are still a few hours of light, but we must rest first, and eat,' said Lief.

'Why?' asked Etta, the only one not buying into this unexpected languidness.

'Because that is the right time,' Lief and Hell both replied and they looked at each other and would have smiled in different circumstances. Something important had changed: it was quite possibly the first time they had agreed about anything. Lief turned back to Etta and favoured him with a grim smile.

'The Gauts think they have beaten us, so they won't be on their guard. Also, they prefer it cold, they come from the far North. The heat will have sapped their strength today, they will have slept – as they wake, they will still be drowsy … and hungry.'

'So what's the plan, Boss?' asked Kran.

And so Lief told them what they needed to hear. No more than that.


Sometime later, they ate in silence, then stood and stretched in that way they'd seen adults do in past lives.

Hell, sword drawn, went first, followed by Nuria, who carried her sling. They staggered their marching formation, scouting ahead as they slipped the secure confines of Vantage by the southern gate that led down to the sea and to an uncertain future.

One of the Gauts had dropped a short sword and Nolly, who was the only one of them strong enough to carry it, took it up in his huge hands. Etta carried a sharpened pole, its point hardened by fire, and Fran and Kran had spent the last part of the afternoon repairing their bows. Lief ambled at the rear feeling like he should be carrying an axe or, at least, a spear: a weapon may have made him feel more secure, but its usefulness was limited.

The crown was quiet for the time being but since its last, pounding burst of power when circlet and sword combined, his thoughts and perceptions had raced.

Nothing escaped his attention.

The air hung heavy amongst the trees as they walked down to shore and sea. Lief could taste the salt tang on his tongue and feel the gentle heartbeat of the waves that folded and flattened as they reached the shore in an exhalation of breath, each one a small death; he felt the rhythm of this old-new land, how ancient shifts and sleight of hand had formed what was sane and safe and somehow *more* – from wood to valley, from hill to shore. Closer, two white moths, like petals, tussled in the last rays of sunlight coming through the trees, as unaware of the coming fury and fire as the banks of nettle and briar. Now that they were at the base of Vantage, by the beach, they turned their tramping north, to darkened reach: of blackened sand, oily pools. They came to Dead Land.

The Gauts' camp crouched hovel windows like empty sockets, staring blind at grey marsh beneath harsh skies. On choppy waters the Gaut ship was taut and to the hilt, sails straining as a hot wind built then blew.

And Lief considered silent Fran … and Lief knew.

Soundless now, they slogged on through muddish water, thoughts on thuggish slaughter. For their enemy slept and, by and by, when they woke it would be to die.

Lief pulled up close to Hell as the others fanned out behind. Near enough to see axes leaned in doorways and darkened forms within, to smell the stench of rotting fish and something ... more grim. Even now, there was no sign of the Little Ones, just the sense of sensible fear. Lief paused and retched – panic rising in his chest, clouding all thoughts save just one that wailed, *this place is vile ... run*!

Then the crown began to burn, and he felt his rage return. The Gauts would pay; they had not woken.

Still he could not see the Little Ones. Still no-one had spoken.

In a whirling blur, Hell darted forward. With a cry of fury, she raised the sword in sinewed arms and scythed. The noise was deafening: the Sword's power and Hell's rage blew the Gaut's crude shelter to sticks and dust.

But nothing stirred, inside the shack was void.

Etta ran forward, into another, Kran and Fran the one next door.

'It's empty!'

'They're all empty,' said Lief. As he'd known they would be.

Like incubi, Gauts burst from mud and tangled reeds, from under soggy marsh that stank decay. With gurgled roar, water spilled from ragged jaw.

The children were trapped: too small, too few. They would be slain by those who slew.

Were it not for Hell.

The sword sang. As the first Gaut came, she grinned quick and twisted in the air: the blade flashed as it shattered axe, sliced hair, then bone.

And, like a stone, the severed head splashed at their feet.

Nuria's sling zipped and Nolly hacked. Hell darted on, sword twirling. And the Gauts, surprise spent, backed, buckled and bent.

This wasn't planned. To fight some would die, I'm not *that* king thought Lief, not now, not ever, NOT I.

'Stop,' he said, but no-one heard.

'Stop!' he cried, just the word. But no-one stopped for no-one heard.

'STOP!' he roared, for death was near: creeping close and quick. And now they paused and turned and saw a sight to make them sick.

A sodden raft slid into view, a sinking wreck with prison crew: Very small children knelt aboard the doomed boat: pinch-faced and perishing. To cut the rope that tied them down would loose the raft and they would drown.

'Stop,' trembled Lief, for that was how his heart felt, 'don't hurt them ...' and he too knelt.

And so, the others.

They'd found the Little Ones. It was almost over.

'That was it, then?' Etta snarled across at Lief, his face mottled with fury, 'that was your great plan to *sneak up on them and rescue the Little Ones*, just like that – that's all you had? You're no king – you're his fool!'

Lief looked around at his subjects? Friends? More than that ... or less? He really didn't know anymore. Fran was staring at him calmly. But the others would not meet his gaze. Even faithful Nolly.

Hell ignored everyone, instead she cursed and glared at the Gauts. One with massive arms and grey green skin stood apart. This was the leader, judging by its size. It strode calmly over to the decapitated corpse of its warrior. Grunting with the effort of hauling the body up, it hurled the torso several arms lengths into the water to float away. The large Gaut then picked up the bleeding head by its matted hair and studied the face, thin drool dripping from needle teeth. Everyone watched in silence.

*Everyone except Lief. All the while he kept his eye on the sinking raft.*

The Trollhaten Beast marched over to Hell where she knelt, and tossed the gory thing in front of her. Hell looked at him, as if to say *so what*. The Gaut gave a short grunt that almost sounded like amusement … then kicked Hell very hard in the stomach. Everyone shouted, as Hell dropped the Sword and doubled over into the mud, choking.

*Everyone except Lief. All the while he kept his eye on the sinking raft. In less than two hundred heartbeats it would sink under the choppy waves.*

The Gaut general barked an order and the other Gauts moved forward and started to tie the hands of the kneeling children. Etta struggled and was also beaten. A smallish Gaut approached Lief, some twine in its gnarled fingers. Its face cracked open in a leer like a scab splitting and Lief caught the reek of rotting fish on its breath. It made to grab Lief's hands roughly but grunted with surprise when they stayed put. It tugged again at his wrists, harder this time and Lief felt the crown's power flex, as if limbering up. His hands did not move, even when the Gaut pulled with all its might and, yet, Lief felt nothing. The others began to turn and look, puzzlement on their faces. All watched the Gaut try and fail to bind a skinny boy's arms.

*Everyone except Lief. All the while he kept his eye on the sinking raft. In less than one hundred heartbeats it would sink under the choppy waves. And, one by one, the Little Ones would start to drown.*

In anger, the Gaut aimed a slap at the side of Lief's head. But somehow the hand missed, as if Lief had veered out of the way. Yet he hadn't moved a muscle. *You were right, in the beginning, to stay off the hill with its old castle and older foe that slept beneath*, thought Lief. With a roar of anger, the Gaut punched Lief with its huge fist clenched and there was a crack and the roar of anger became an animal yelp of pain. Everyone watched as the Gaut raised its mangled hand that dripped blood through splintered bone.

*Everyone except Lief. All the while he kept his eye on the sinking raft. In less than fifty heartbeats it would sink under the choppy waves. And, one by one, the Little Ones would start to drown. Their hands were tied.*

143

The Gaut commander knew a challenge when it saw one and strode over to where Lief knelt meekly. Passing a hovel, it picked up a double-headed axe and swung the weapon at Lief's head. *You should never have come up the hill, you should have let us be.* Everyone watched as the axe turned into an eagle that screeched and flew from the surprised Gaut's hands.

*Everyone except Lief. All the while he kept his eye on the sinking raft. In under twenty heartbeats it would sink under the choppy waves. And, one by one, the Little Ones would start to drown. Their hands were tied. But there was still time ... just.*

The Gauts now rushed at Lief, as one, aiming kicks and punches that never seemed to connect. And Lief had a vision of permafrost and lava meeting in a landscape choked with noise and swirling mist. *You are not of here – you are of ice and rock – this land is ash and oak, warm summers, soft hills and gentle rivers ... and something that sleeps, even you beasts would fear.* Everyone watched as the Gauts fell back, panting.

*Everyone except Lief. All the while he kept his eye on the sinking raft. It was almost under the choppy waves.*

*It was time.*

You do not belong, he thought. Lief concentrated every thought on the crown and on the deep presence he had felt since the first day when they arrived. He felt the scale that clad and sinew bound stir, and he concentrated harder, until his head felt as if it would split with the pressure from the crown.

*… deep in caverns leagues below, a huge eyelid opened the width of a hair. The brawn that bound the bone of the precious land flexed.*

Lief finally turned to Fran. 'Say it,' he said.

And Fran, who had not spoken for many moons, looked about, as if seeing the scene about them for the first time and whispered, 'Wake,' as Lief rose and ran to the raft to save the Little Ones … and the Gauts heard the muted roar of a monster far more terrible than them.

The warm wind blew harder, the dragon's breath rose as thick as fog from the sea and the Gauts howled in fear.

## Chapter 11: Horizons

[BARD]
*Now my song draws to a close,*
*And like the tides, it ebbs and flows.*
*Evil beaten, fortunes rise,*
*Fellowship lightens troubled skies.*

*But the gods look on with knowing eyes*

*When endless land became sea and shore,*
*Courageous destiny rose once more.*
*Children saved, Trollhaten dies,*
*For the Age of Man is on the rise.*

*But the gods look on with jealous eyes.*

The smoke-laden fog blew away. Its departure revealed the Gauts gone. Or there, but they had now returned to their first form: misshapen stones, standing in the evening sun like sentinels – as if guarding the marshes – the gateway to the land they had tried to invade that had been their downfall.

The crown had showed Lief what he had to do, what he could do. The Leviathan that lay beneath the bedrock of Vantage had stirred and not woken, but that had been enough. Its deadly breath had rolled out across the land – its land – and the invaders had no power over what could not be frightened or fought.

'What about the others?' Hell had asked Lief as he stood at the prow of the captured Gaut ship deep in thought. 'The ones who marched inland?' Lief closed his eyes and concentrated. The crown was quiet now and he had the feeling it would stay that way for a while. He still had his visions but they were fading.

'The same thing happened to them …' he could see doubt in Hell's eyes, so he fished about for an explanation, ' … the fog went a long way.'

Lief was glad that he and Hell were talking again – it was stupid, but it almost made him feel better than defeating the Gauts – a process he wasn't convinced he fully understood.

'And thank you,' he said, turning to Hell. She looked happy but still asked;

'Whatever for?'

'I'd be dead if it wasn't for you. Several times, probably.'

'Happy to help, Your Grace,' she favoured Lief with a quick, ironic smile. 'Lief the Illustrious.'

'No, just Lief is fine.'

'I'll leave you alone, you looked like you were enjoying your own thoughts … as usual,' said Hell. 'You probably haven't noticed, but Nuria and the others don't like this ship as much as you seem to … it doesn't hold good memories. You can think up a name for it whilst you stand at the pointy end looking all noble and a bit smug – you almost deserve it.' And Lief was so surprised he nearly asked her to stay.

Kran had been right; the ship virtually sailed itself.

It was a short journey around the coast to their beach and Lief noted that the others did seem relieved to be back on dry land. They walked up the winding hill, using the path Hell and Lief had climbed what seemed like a lifetime ago.

To all intents, it was a lifetime. Was that how it would seem from now on? Was life not one life but dozens, even hundreds of different lives strung together by events that changed you? Lief had no idea … but he'd think about it later.

If the Little Ones had been traumatised by their ordeal with the Trollhaten Beasts, they did a good job of hiding it. Most of them ran ahead shouting and laughing.

'I think when you are really small, you are strong in different ways,' said Nuria. And Lief nodded. He was about to ask a question, but she had moved on to walk with Hell – as usual.

Instead, Lief dropped back to where Fran, Kran, Etta and Nolly walked and chatted. He said very little but he caught Kran's eye whilst Fran was talking to Etta. Fran had the same accent as her sister, but she was softer-spoken and hesitant after so long mute. Kran gave Lief a grin and mouthed *thanks*.

[LIEF]
*Life, at times, is pretty shit,*
*And it's fair to moan a bit.*
*Stuff happens and it can be tragic*
*- it all won't stop (as if by magic).*
*That's why it's good to take the time,*
*To fathom fun is not a crime.*
*So never let a prospect pass,*
*To relax and have a laugh.*

Urgh! Lief was well-aware he needed to work on his recitations … but the Cauldron, for its part at least, rose to the occasion and produced a rich meaty stew with onions and wild garlic in a tangy broth that must have been slightly fermented as they soon felt light-headed and giggly.

Then sleepy.

One by one, they became quieter and lay down by the fire to sleep the rest of the short night by the light of the dying embers.

Lief waited, studying each face, relocating this perfect moment to memory. He lingered longest on Hell, who slept with the Little Ones burrowed against her, the flames lighting features that could be sharp when she was out to fight the world, or prove something to herself but transformed when she smiled … or looked at him. These days. Sometimes. Then, Lief had to admit to himself, Hell was the most beautiful and surprising person he knew.

Studying her gave him a not-unpleasant ache somewhere in his chest like his heart was being gently tugged from the protective shell of his ribcage. But a greater pull, a sense of something undone that wouldn't fade, made him rise and steal away just before dawn.

For now, they did not need him: they needed Hell with her passion and fury, her compassion and her commitment to finding the Treasures. For now, he had a ship with no name, a country with no land and a family somewhere. He would try and find all three, then he would return to the place his heart was already calling home.

For so long he'd had every reason to leave, now he had every reason to come back.

[LIEF]
*What am I to be now?*

He murmured as he walked down the dark path towards the sea and the ashen shades of dawn that slid like a cat between the trees. The crown still sat on his head – he would be a bit lost without it, he suspected. But it didn't really answer his question.

*A grim King with terrible rages,*
*A commanding King, a rock of ages?*
*No King – perhaps a Knave, a Fool?*
*A King of nothing much at all!*

*Sympathy is well and good,*
*It's Love that counts*
                *– and so it should.*

*So King who cares, a King of sighs?*
*A King to brighten tender eyes?*

*King of pomp, a King of glamour?*
*A bejewelled King in dazzling armour?*

*Admiration is well and good,*
*It's Love that counts*
                    *– and so it should.*

*A King of cares, a King of giving,*
*No King of Quests, but a King for living!*
*For sacrifice is well and good*
*But it's Love that counts*
                    *– and so it should.*


It was a shame no-one heard – for once his words felt like they hit the mark. Hell would have nodded, in that way of hers. He hoped. It was her approval above all others that he would seek until the end.

He couldn't imagine a world without her in it and he hoped with all his heart she would forgive him.


*I would spin for you a fleece,*
*From the shafts of golden sun on sea.*
*But all I have to offer you*
*Is what becomes of me.*

His nameless ship slipped anchor and swung towards his old home – or whatever might remain of that land with its endless grass and scattered settlements, its fond memories and familiar faces – all of which demanded answers. But as it did so, he turned for one last look at Vantage and the sight of it in the early light, crumbling but proud, cushioned by the soft foliage on the hill, almost made him turn back.

And Hell watched him go.

*I love you,* they both said on the very same pulse of their hearts. But their words, like their destiny, were swept away by the beat of the waves.

THE END

About the author

When Robin grew up, he thought he wanted to be a cavalry officer until everyone else realised that putting him in charge of a tank was a very bad idea. He then became an assistant gravedigger in London. After that he had a career frantically starting businesses (everything from dog-sitting to cigars, tuition to translation)... until finally settling down to write improbable stories to keep his children from killing each other on long car journeys.

Robin plays most sports. Poorly.

Printed in Great Britain
by Amazon

20386039R00089